ISBN: 978-1-7751026-4-9

I0601818

Dedication

This book is dedicated to all those who have been through a storm, who have felt the power of God work in a quiet way or a mighty way to calm the storm without or within.

The Storm

Haven of Rest Trilogy

Book 1

by

Ronna Bacon

Verses to Remember

Matthew 11:28
Come to Me, all *you* who labor and are
heavy laden, and I will give you rest.

Mark 5:39, 40
39 Then He arose and rebuked the wind, and
said to the sea, "Peace, be still!" And the
wind ceased and there was a great
calm. **40** But He said to them, "Why are you
so fearful? How *is it* that you have no
faith?"

Table of Contents

Prologue

He watched from the sidelines as she handed over her boarding pass and then walked onto the plane. He followed and found his seat two rows back and on the other side. It would be a long flight, he knew, but she was going nowhere he couldn't see her.

It was a long twelve hours later that their flight landed. He was tired and ready to go home but first he had to follow her and find out where the information was he had to retrieve. He had been given word from the streets she had it in her possession.

He watched once again as she retrieved her luggage and then headed for a taxi. His friend was waiting for him and they quickly followed. But it was strange. She was not headed for her home town. Instead, she was heading to the next terminal that local flights flew from. This changed everything. He had to scramble to get in line behind her to find out where she was going. By the time he had reached the counter, the flight was full and he was turned away. He cursed to himself. This was not going the way it should. Reluctantly he booked a seat on the next flight, that left in the morning. She would already be on the ground there for twenty-four hours by the time he arrived. He shared a look with his companion. This was not good. The one who had hired him and sent him overseas to that worn-torn country to follow her and retrieve that information was not going to be pleased. He really didn't want to be the one to tell that person.

He watched as the small plane took off into the night sky. Soon the lights had disappeared. He hoped it was not a sign that's what would happen to him if he failed.

Chapter 1

Frankie Brennan was tired and worn out. The years of being a street cop and undercover for many of them had taken their toll on his body, mind and spirit. He had tried to resign, but Caleb Logan, the town Police Chief, had refused to accept it. Instead, he had suggested Frankie take some vacation time and sort things through.

Frankie looked around the church entry and wondered why he was there. Ben Johnson, a fellow police officer, had looked at him one day during the past week and told him to be here this morning. Frankie had taken a look at him, hesitated and then agreed. He knew he needed something to change but he wasn't sure how he was ever going to find his way back to what he had been. That man was gone, he was sure.

He turned as he felt a little girl race by him, gold ringlets flying. He thought she was maybe three, but she went by so quick he wasn't sure. He listened to what she was saying.

"Miss Dee, Miss Dee. You're here. You're really here."

A young woman who had been standing near him turned at the sound of the child's voice. A smile broke out and she bent to gather the little one into her arms. The little girl ended up nose to nose with her as she hugged her.

"I am?" she asked. "I am really, really, really here?"

The little one's head bobbed up and down quickly. "You are, you are. And you have to sit with me."

"No, really, I do?" At the vigorous head nod, she smiled again. "Okay, I guess I do. Let's go find your Mom."

Frankie watched as she walked away, the child in her arms. A touch on his shoulder and he turned. Ben was standing there watching him, a look in his eye that Frankie had trouble reading.

"Come on, Frankie. Let's go find Marg. She said she would save a seat for us at the back."

Frankie was uncomfortable waiting for the service to start. It had been too long and things seemed too different now. Marg reached over and patted his hand.

"Relax," she said. "They won't ask you to take part in anything this week."

He shot her a wide-eyed look.

"They'll wait until next week." She looked at him, face straight but a twinkle in her eye.

He narrowed his eyes at her, then responded, "Do you think they would wait another week?"

She laughed softly. "Frankie, you'll be fine."

As the service was starting, the young woman he had seen in the entry passed the end of their row of chairs. She lightly touched Ben on the shoulder who looked up and smiled. He went to stand to let her in and she shook her head and pointed to another row. He sat back down and watched her.

The hair on Frankie's neck bristled. Something was happening. He knew that feeling from the streets. There was evil in the building. He shot a quick look around but couldn't pinpoint anyone in particular. He would have to have a talk with Ben when church was over.

But he never got a chance to speak with Ben. With a muttered word to Marg, Ben had left before the end of the service. Marg mentioned to Frankie that sometimes people in the church needed help at the end of service and Ben was one of the men who always volunteered.

Frankie looked around once again. He still had that feeling, he knew it only too well. Who was it?

Ben met Frankie the next morning for coffee. At this point, Frankie was convinced that he may have imagined the feeling and didn't pursue it.

"Caleb mentioned that he had suggested you look into working at the youth centre." Ben watched his young friend, trying to gauge his reaction and thoughts.

Frankie hesitated before speaking. "He did, Ben. I'm not sure though that's what I want to do." Frankie stared at his coffee cup. "I'm not sure what I really want."

Ben nodded. He figured that was how Frankie was feeling. "Why don't we head over there and you can get a feel for how it runs and what would be expected. They really need a man who can work with the young men and be a mentor to them."

Frankie snorted. "Like I can do that?"

Ben stopped him from continuing. "You're beat up right now, down in spirit and heart. You have no idea what you want to do, whether you want to continue as an officer or go into something different. Your faith has taken a real beating in the last few months, if not years." Ben hesitated, not sure how his next words would be accepted. "You hide it well, Frankie. I know you were in love with Ashling." Frankie's eyes shot to his. "Not too many people know that. I know you well. That's how I knew."

Frankie stared out the window at the parking lot. "I was. But Liam is the one she needs." He stopped, swallowed, and then continued, "I don't know if I will ever find that one for me."

"God knows, Frankie, God knows exactly who you need. Have patience." Ben pulled out some money for their coffee and stood. "Come with me. We'll head for the youth centre. It's not that far, you can come back for your truck."

As they entered the youth centre, they could hear voices from the gym. Ben took a look at Frankie, then headed that way. They stopped just inside the door.

The young woman Frankie had observed in the church stood there, in jeans, soft jade sweater, sneakers and with her shoulder length brown hair swinging loose. In front of her stood a youth of about 14, switchblade in hand.

Frankie made a move to go forward, but a hand on his arm stopped. Ben shook his head and motioned for him to wait.

"Peter, you know the rules. No weapons in the centre and that is a weapon." Her voice was soft and calm, her stance relaxed.

The youth looked at the knife and then at her. He shook his head and clicked the knife open and shut. "No one takes my knife, Miss D. No one."

She tilted her head and looked at him. "Well, here we do." The fingers on her extended hand wiggled. "Now, let's have it.

You know we have certain rules for everyone, and weapons are one of them."

He shook his head but was starting to look uncertain.

She looked at the ceiling, sighed and then looked back at him. "Peter, I have had some real tough guys hassle me. I have been threatened with kitchen knives, machetes, switchblades, revolvers, rifles, semi and automatic weapons. I have had bombs explode not far from me. I have been targeted in ways you will never know and by men and boys tougher than you. Now, the knife."

Peter sneered. "Yeah, right. You're just saying that. When would someone like you ever have been threatened like that?"

She sighed again, then spoke, her voice too low for the men to catch her words. Peter's eyes began to grow round, his mouth dropped open, and then his hand slackened on the knife. She reached for it and took it gently from him.

"Next time, Peter, leave these at home. You don't want the problems that will come if you don't."

Peter's mouth opened and closed a few times as he stared at her. Then he turned and ran past the men. Frankie turned to watch him.

Ben walked up to the young woman and then stood by her side, watching as she flicked the knife open and closed. Frankie approached them slowly, not sure what to expect. So far, it had been an interesting introduction to the youth centre.

Ben finally sighed, held out his hand, and she dropped the knife into it. He stared at the ceiling. "Still bullying the boys are you, Deirdre? At least this time, you didn't drop him in his tracks and disarm him that way."

She shoved him with her shoulder, Frankie watching in amazement as she did so. "Behave, Benny, or I'll tell Marg you're being bad again."

Ben laughed, then asked, "So, who taught you again?"

She shook her head as she turned to look at him. "You know well who. My uncle." She patted his cheek. "Right, Uncle Benny?"

Ben threw his head back and laughed at her nonsense, then hugged her. "So glad you're home safe from overseas. But then I see this and think maybe you might be safer over there."

She stood back, hands on his arms, and studied him. "Funny you should say that. I've had that feeling again in the last few days."

Ben sobered. "And you didn't say anything?"

"Ben, stop. A feeling isn't enough to go on." She looked over at Frankie. "Are you going to introduce me to your friend, or does he have to listen to you berate me?"

Ben just shook his head. "You know your family wants you to be safe. Being here is a concession to that."

She grimaced. "I know and I hate that."

She turned to Frankie and held out her hand. "Ben's being too bossy to introduce us. I'm Deirdre McNabb. Ben's a relative in case you missed that."

Frankie shook her hand. "Frankie Brennan."

He watched as she tilted her head and studied him through hazel eyes. She shook her head. "No, what's your full name? Frankie doesn't suit."

His eyes widening in shock, he looked past her at Ben, who was trying hard not to laugh. He stammered, "It's Franklin, but no one calls me that but my Mom."

She thought about that, then shook her head. "Nope, that won't work. The kids here will eat you alive with that name. We'll come up with something."

She turned and walked out the door, Ben trailing behind her. He turned and looked back at Frankie, who was just standing there, staring.

"Come along, Franklin." Ben's smile widened. "It will be interesting to see what name she comes up with."

"You didn't warn me, Ben. You should have."

"What would be the fun in that?" Ben started to laugh again. "By the way, she's the one who runs the centre." Ben laughed harder as Frankie stopped, mouth dropping open, and stared at him.

Chapter 2

Frankie had been at the centre for a week. He was still trying to wrap his head around the scene he had seen when Ben had walked him into the building. Deirdre was loved by all the youths and seemed to be everywhere. He was still waiting for her to come up with a name for him and it would be interesting when she did.

He stood late that Friday afternoon near the front desk, waiting for Deirdre or Miss D as the youth called her to come from her office. They had agreed to a dinner meeting to discuss his tasks. He watched as an older well dressed gentleman came in and looked around. He stopped at the desk and while Frankie couldn't hear his words, he watched the young woman he was talking to. Something just didn't seem right, and he approached them.

"Can I help you with something?"

The man turned, his eyes narrowed as he looked Frankie up and down, shook his head and walked out.

"What was that about?" Frankie asked the girl, Amy he thought.

"I don't know. It was really strange. He wanted to know about Miss D and whether she was around and when she was or wasn't." She looked at Frankie. "I didn't tell."

"I know you didn't. If you ever had anyone like that again, excuse yourself and come find me. I'll deal with them."

Amy continued to watch him, then said, "I'm glad you're here. That's not the first time someone has come in like that asking about Miss D. In fact, there was one the other day..." Her voice died away. "The one the other day had an accent. I don't know what though."

Frankie nodded. "Just find me."

He turned as Deirdre came up behind him.

She studied him for a minute, then looked at the door. "All set?" she asked.

"I am if you are." Frankie held the door for her.

"What was that all about?" she asked as they walked towards the down town area.

Frankie shook his head. "I'm really not sure. Amy said someone was questioning her about your hours. I told her to call me next time."

Deirdre shook her head. "You're not around all the time."

"I know, but when I am, that will be part of my job."

Deirdre looked frustrated but waited to speak until they had been seated in the town's Italian restaurant. "Frankie, you mean well, but in case you missed it, I have been all over the world and in many war-torn areas and trouble spots. That's what I do. It's who I am. I can take care of myself. And I can't do that if I am smothered."

Frankie sat back and thought about what she had said. "I apologize. I should have talked to you first. I realize you have been all over but please understand, protecting people is who I am."

She laid her hand on his folded hands. "I understand. Part of why I really didn't want to move here is because Ben can smother. He doesn't mean to but he can. My parents have finally realized I can take care of myself but Ben still sees the little girl I was. My experiences have changed me to some extent, I think, just like yours have changed you."

Frankie went to speak but stopped when she glanced around the restaurant, with an almost frightened look on her face.

"What's wrong?"

"I don't know but for the last ten days or so since I came back I have felt like I was being followed. I haven't been able to pinpoint anyone though. I never had this feeling overseas, just once I was on the plane coming back."

Frankie looked around, noting faces. "I have had the same feeling when I am around you. I felt it at your church the first Sunday I was there."

She shivered as she listened to him. "That's getting a little too close for comfort. Don't tell Ben, he'll smother me more than he already does."

He started to shake his head, then watched her face. Against his better judgement, he nodded.

As they walked back towards their vehicles in the dusk, Frankie kept an eye on their surroundings. Something was off and he couldn't figure out just what. Movement to their right caught his attention, and he pulled Deirdre over and behind him. A blow to his head sent him to his knees. He heard angry words as he tried to stay on his knees and break through the blackness that threatened to engulf him.

He felt hands on his arms and a voice calling to him. He shook his head and then wondered why he did such a stupid thing.

He was finally able to focus enough to see Deirdre before him, concern on her face.

"What happened?" he muttered.

"Strangest thing. That thug walloped you, asked me where something was, and then just took off."

"Help me up." Frankie staggered a bit as he came to his feet. "Did you get a look at him?"

"Tall, thin, jeans, hoodie, dress shoes - what thug wears dress shoes anyway - couldn't see hair or eyes, but I have his voice imprinted on my memory."

Frankie studied her.   No, it didn't make sense.   What had he wanted and why did he think she had it?

"Do you have any idea of what he was after?"

She shook her head. "Not a one. And do not tell Ben. He won't let me walk alone even in the daylight if you do."

Frankie grinned at her.   "I wouldn't want to meet you in a dark alley.   You're scary."

She shoved him, and then grabbed his arm to help him balance.   "Shh. No one's supposed to know that."

They turned once more to walk to their vehicles, Frankie catching her hand in his. To his surprise, she made no effort to remove it.

"It is strange. We'll figure it out."

"Right," she said, "somehow, some place, somewhere.   I just don't like the feeling I'm being watched.   It's very unnerving."

Frankie stopped by her car and turned to watch her. She was calm and peaceful in her stance but he caught the uncertainty and a bit of fear in her eyes. She turned her eyes to him and caught him staring at her.

"Be careful, Franklin, I can put you down before you could even blink."

He laughed. "I understand that you can, Ben's been talking." He sobered. "I just don't want you to get hurt. And not on my watch. I don't want to answer to Ben or even Marg." He shuddered dramatically.

"Well, then, I guess we won't tell them." She turned to lean against her car. "Can I ask you something, Frankie?" At his nod, she continued, "What are you planning to do now that you're not sure you want to continue as a police officer?"

He leaned his hip against the car and once again studied her face. He sighed. "Deirdre, I really don't know. Working the streets and especially the last bit with Ashling and Liam, it really took a toll on me. My heart needs to be refreshed. I need to find my way back to God and my faith certainly needs strengthening. Right now, I feel like I am in a huge storm that has no end."

She nodded. "I can understand that. I have had some others say that to me but it hasn't been as strong as what you say." She stopped, and tilting her head, watched him. "I do know that Jesus calmed that storm on Galilee. If He can calm a storm like that, how He must be able to calm the storms in our souls. What are you willing to give or do to find that peace and comfort in your life?"

Frankie thought about that. "You ask hard questions, Miss D. That gives me a lot of think about."

"First Frankie, humble yourself, get down on your knees, and just open your heart. Just listen. Listening is hard. As humans, we want to be the ones talking. With God, we need to listen first. The path He asks you to walk through the storm to the peace on the other side may be a lot harder than anything you have ever done before."

Frankie hesitated, then spoke, "That sounds like personal experience."

She turned to unlock her car. "It is. One day, I'll tell you about it. It's not real pretty."

Frankie held her door for her and before he shut it, he spoke. "Thanks for taking time for dinner. I enjoyed tonight, well except for that little bit near the alley. And thank you for being bold with your words. You may just have reached through the storm to me."

He thought he saw tears glinting in her eyes but her voice was steady. "I have been praying for you. Go home, Frankie, spend time on your knees."

He nodded, then watched her drive away. As he climbed into his truck, he saw headlights pull away from the curb and follow her. That's not right, he thought, and pulled his truck up behind the vehicle. He followed it and then it suddenly veered away. He didn't like that one bit. He followed Deirdre to make sure she was home safe and then parked his truck at the curb. He had time to watch and wait.

Chapter 3

A tap at his window awakened him. He stretched then looked over at the passenger window. Deirdre stood there, hands on hips, frown on her face.

He turned the ignition on enough so he could lower the window on her side. "Morning," he said, voice gruff.

"What are you doing here?" She demanded. She was not pleased with him, he could tell. "Go home, Frankie. I don't need you playing babysitter."

He turned off the truck and scrambled out to go after her as she set off down the sidewalk.

"Deirdre, wait." She stopped as he came up behind her. "You were followed last night when you left work. The car broke off when I came up behind it, but it was definitely after you."

Her posture was stiff and straight. She didn't answer him.

He came around to stand in front of her. She had a closed, shuttered look on her face. "Did you hear what I said?"

Her hazel raised to him and he caught a glint of something he couldn't read. "Go home, Frankie. As I said, I don't need a babysitter." She brushed by him and continued down the street.

Hand on his head, he stared after her. Really? He told her she was followed and then she brushed it and him off? He ran to catch up with her.

"Go away, Frankie."

He pulled her to a stop. "No, I won't, Deirdre. Someone is following you. I won't let anything happen to you."

She spun and stared at him and then just shook her head. "No, don't try. I don't need a rescuer. It won't work, you know." He stared at her, puzzlement on his face. "I won't be a replacement." She poked him in the chest. "You need to figure out what you want and where you're going, and that you have to do on your own. I won't be part of it."

She strode away, leaving him standing staring after her. Did he just totally blow it with her, he wondered? He turned to do as she ask, but his instincts was telling him differently and he turned back.

As he turned back, he saw a car pull up beside her and a man step out. Deirdre had stopped and then stepped back from him. Frankie saw the man reach for her arm to pull her towards the car. He wasn't close enough, he thought, as he ran towards them.

Deirdre was not happy with Frankie and her mind was on the confrontation she had just had with him. She wasn't paying as particular attention to her surroundings as she normally did. The car stopping and the man exiting startled her and she stepped back. When he reached for her arm, she stepped back further. She shook her head and when he persisted, she stepped back further. She could hear running footsteps coming up. That had to be Frankie, she thought. He's too far away yet.

She reached for the man's wrist and with a little flurry of moves that would have made her friends from the streets overseas proud, she had him on the ground. Frankie slid to a stop beside her.

"Yep, I really wouldn't want to meet you in a dark alley." He reached down and hauled the man to his feet.

"Okay, mister. What's your problem? Why are you bothering this lady?"

The man, clothes dusty from the streets, brushed himself off. "I was just asking for directions and she attacked me."

"Sorry, buddy. That's not what happened. You would have had her in your vehicle if she hadn't made those moves, and by the way, I really want to learn those moves. So how about it? Tell us the truth and exactly why you tried to abduct her."

The man, in his late 30s Frankie figured, stared at him, then with a sudden movement, shoved him towards Deirdre and then was gone. Frankie watched in disgust as the man's car sped off.

"I didn't even get the plate number," he muttered.

A voice beside him quoted it. He spun and looked at her. She shrugged and then repeated it.

"How do you do that?" he demanded. "You would have made a good officer."

She shrugged. "I always have had a good memory."

He turned her around towards her home. "Come on, let's go get some breakfast. And if I see Eddie or Caleb, I'll pass on that number. No, I won't go to Ben. I promise."

"Thank you, Frankie. I appreciate that." She sighed and looked up at the brilliant blue sky. "I'm thinking I will have to tell you my story before long. I just can't shake you, can I?"

He smiled and shook his head. "No, I don't think you can. You're my friend and I don't let friends go." To himself, he added, and you are one of those friends I want in my life forever.

He seated her in a booth at SueEllen's cafe and looked around. Saturday morning meant that a lot of his friends would be here for breakfast. He saw Caleb entering with his family and stood to go towards him, excusing himself from Deirdre.

Caleb Logan stepped to one side after a word to his wife. Hannah smiled and greeted Frankie, then directed the two boys to a table.

"Frankie." Caleb waited. "I know this isn't just a social hello. I can tell. You have your working face on."

Frankie blew out a breath. "It's not. I wish it was. We need to talk sometime soon, Caleb. Something's going on with Deirdre. She was almost abducted this morning." Caleb looked at him, startled, then waited for him to continue. "I don't know how she did it but she had the man down before I caught up to her. She even managed to get the plate number." He shook his head. "She really didn't need my help."

Caleb snorted. "No, she wouldn't. Ben has trained her well, and with her trips overseas, she has picked up a lot more about self defence. I wish I could get her to agree to teach our young women some of her moves."

His eyes drifted to where Deirdre sat, a calm look on her face, watching them. "Why don't you bring her over for supper? Say around 4?"

"Hannah won't mind?"

"No. And neither will Seth or Noah. She teaches them in Sunday school sometimes and they adore her."

"All right. I'll check with her. If she can't, I'll be there."

Caleb moved away to join his family as Frankie slid back into the booth across from Deirdre. Her eyes moved from him to Caleb and back to him again.

"Okay, so what time is it you planned for me to meet with Caleb?"

He looked at her, astonished, then began to laugh. "How do you do that?"

"Do what?" she smirked.

"Figure out what was said across the room from you."

"Lip reading. I have friends who are deaf and they taught me."

"You really are scary, you know." Frankie grabbed up a menu. "Let's eat. All this activity has made me hungry."

She shook her head. "Men and boys - always a bottomless pit when it comes to food."

As they left the cafe, Deirdre stopped him with a hand on his arm. "Go home, Frankie. I have things I need to do, and you have to let me."

He nodded. "Can I pick you up about 3:30 to go to Caleb's?"

She sighed, then nodded. "If you must."

"I must."

She pulled a face, then said, "You're smothering me, Frankie. Don't. I will walk away and leave." At that, she turned and walked away from him.

He watched her leave, knowing he would see her later. Right now, he had some research he needed to do and headed home.

****

The Watcher stood across from the cafe, eyes on the two. He followed Frankie with his gaze until he saw he was headed away from Deirdre, then he shoved on his sunglasses and sauntered down the street after Deirdre, all the world like a tourist in town just for the day. He would follow her and when the time was right, he would find that information he needed. Time was running short but he couldn't rush this. If he did, many more than just this one woman would pay.

Chapter 4

Frankie sat back from his computer and stared at the screen. He had never expected to find the information that he had by putting Deirdre's name into a search engine. He really didn't know how to absorb what he was reading.

He knew she had been all over the world, into troubled areas, but he didn't know that it had been through a mission that her parents had set up when she was a child. The Recovering People Mission sent aid and people into troubled areas of the world, war-torn areas, areas where natural and manmade disasters had struck. From what he was reading, Deirdre had been on many of those missions in the last few years.

He paused and wondered if this was what she had meant when she said she had a story to tell and it wasn't pretty.

As he looked back to his screen, it refreshed and a news article popped up. He pulled it up to read. His hands on the top of head, he read it through and then again. Deirdre - that explained why her name was different from her uncle and her father. He leaned forward and read the article again and then searched for more.

A sudden look at the clock and he knew he had to leave. He shut down his computer and stood. He had to be so careful that she didn't read him and that he had learned what lurked in her background.

He grabbed his keys and headed for his truck, eyes scanning the area out of habit. His eyes narrowed as he targeted in on a car parked across the street from his house. No one was around it, but he didn't recognize it. Out of habit, he got the plate number and wrote it down. He would pass it on later.

He knocked at Deirdre's door. As he waited, he again scanned the area. He didn't see anything but he had that creeping feeling that he was being watched and closely. He turned in a circle but saw nothing. So what was it?

Deirdre unlocked the door and beckoned him in. She returned to her dining room table, that was covered in papers.

"Okay, I'm back. So what is the situation over there?"

As a man spoke, Frankie realized she was on a speaker phone.

"Phil and Terry are headed out tonight, should be on the ground there tomorrow. Cal is already there. Communication is spotty at best given the infrastructure destruction. That cyclone hit hard."

"I know. The equipment and supplies are headed out when?"

"Some are already on the way. Those we could ship from the warehouse in Australia. Danny says what we can send from here will go tomorrow. He's working on getting the cargo plane loaded today, he'll grab some sleep, and then head out."

"Sounds good." Frankie noticed her rubbing her forehead. She had a headache and was beginning to look a bit stressed, unusual for her. "Where do you need me most?"

"Right now, here. Right here with your Mom and the other board members. I'll be heading out tonight if I can catch the right flight. You've been there. You know the area and the people. We need your expertise to direct us where we need to be working. I'm not sending you back there."

Deirdre stopped her pacing and stared at the floor, arms wrapped around her. Frankie watched, not sure how he should react or if he even should. She looked up and he saw the shimmer of the tears she refused to let fall.

"That's fine. I can't go back there. Ever. And it hurts. I can't get a flight tonight or even tomorrow. Not a direct flight and I'm not comfortable with layovers."

"It's not that far of a drive. I could send Timothy but I need him here directing the warehouse."

"I know, Dad, I know. I'll figure something out and let you know."

"I know you will, pumpkin. You always do." Her father's voice hesitated, then he spoke, "Well, we've made what plans we can for now. Let's have a word of prayer, DeeDee, before we say goodbye.'

Frankie's head went down automatically when the deep bass voice began his prayer. He felt a hand on his and grasped Deirdre's hand.

When she raised her hand, he could see that she had closed down part of herself again and steeled herself for what only she knew was ahead.

She looked at him, then at her table. "I need to put this paperwork in my briefcase and then pack a bag. Somehow or other, I have to get on the road tonight."

"What about the youth centre?" Frankie asked as she stacked the paperwork.

"I've called Peter. He'll take over for now. Unless you're volunteering?"

"No way." Frankie shook his head. "How be I be your chauffeur?"

She spun to look at him and began to shake her head.

"Listen to me. It will be late at night, you're already feeling like you're being followed, and I know you are. If I drive, it will throw them off hopefully. You can rest, catch some sleep, and be ready to go in the morning." He paused, then said, "Just where are we heading anyway?"

She started to laugh. "Franklin, what am I to do with you?" As he opened his mouth, she held up a finger. "No, don't answer that. I don't know if I really want your answer."

He began to laugh. "You do leave yourself open at times, you know."

She giggled. "I know. Now wait here. I'm going to grab my ready pack and throw in a few things." She spoke over her shoulder as she headed for her bedroom, "If you're going, we'll need to stop and grab your stuff. Answer that, will you?"

Frankie answers her phone.

"Hello? Who's this?"

Frankie recognized her father's voice. "My name is Frankie. I'm a friend of Deirdre."

"Frankie? Well, well." He could hear something in her father's voice, and he turned to gaze down the hallway. What had she said? "That Frankie. Now, I feel better, knowing you're with her. I'm going to be honest and tell you something that has me bothered. I can't warn DeeDee. She needs protection. We just got a warning here at headquarters that she is being sought by some nationals from another country. They think she has brought back information somehow with her from her last trip that if known would bring down a corrupt portion of a government. She has no idea that this is going on. Stick with her, son. Don't let her out of your sight." Her father paused. "Now, if she's not in the room with you, tell her that I don't want her to come until at least Monday. I'm not getting out of here before Sunday night, Monday morning at the earliest."

Frankie continued to watch down the hall. "I will. I will also guard your daughter with my life if necessary."

Her father paused, then said, voice roughened with emotion, "Thank you. I pray it doesn't come to that. You're good for her. Ask her about her story sometime. You two are a fit. Ben's been talking."

The phone clicked in his ear, and he lowered the phone he held in his hand, standing there lost in thought. He started as a soft hand reached out and took it. He looked up. Deirdre stood there, watching him.

"It must have been Dad. He has that effect on people."

Frankie studied the woman ahead of him. He knew she was around his age, late 20s, early 30s. She was beautiful in his opinion. She was exactly what he had been looking for in a girl friend and maybe a wife. He had to be very careful that he didn't blow it, though, and he could very easily, given what he knew.

"Yeah, it was. He called to let you know you didn't need to come tonight. He can't get a flight before tomorrow night or Monday morning. He said you didn't to be there until Monday."

She shook her head. "I'll go tomorrow."

He stopped her with a hand on her arm. "We'll go tomorrow." At her look, he repeated, "We'll go tomorrow, unless you would like to head out after supper with Caleb and Hannah. It's not that far. We could be there by late tonight."

She stood and watched him, reading his face. She nodded and he reached for her bag and briefcase. Waiting for her to lock up her house, he again studied the area, looking for what he didn't know but her father had explained a lot. He now knew the danger but where it would come from or how, that was still the unknown.

He tucked her bags in the back of his truck, then helped her in and shut the door behind her. Rounding the front of the truck, he stopped and once again looked over the area. Someone was there, he could feel the eyes.

After a quick stop back at his place, he pulled up in front of Caleb's house. He laid a hand on her arm as she undid her seat belt.

"Wait a minute, Deirdre." She turned to look at him. "We still need to talk at some point about the danger you're in. We can't run from it forever."

"There's no we in it, Frankie." She stared at him, defying him.

"No, there is a we. I got involved by being there last night. I'm involved, whether you like it or not. You are not facing whatever is going on by yourself. I don't let my friends go through trouble alone. Go talk to anyone on the street. Talk to Ashling and Liam." He brought his hand up and brushed her hair back from her face. "No, I'm not going anywhere. And don't try to run. It won't work. I'll find you."

She shook her head. "Not if I have anything to say about it." She turned to look at Caleb's house. "Come. We need to go in. Let's put this aside from now."

She was out of the truck and halfway up the walk before he could respond. He hurried to catch up with her, stopping her just as she went to ring the doorbell.

"Our discussion is not over." He stared at her and she refused to look away. "It's not. We'll take it up again later."

Neither one had heard the door open. Caleb stood watching them, then shook his head. Here we go again, he thought.

"Would you two like to come in or just stand out here all night and stare at one another?" His amused tone broke through the silence.

Frankie flushed and tried to come up with some words.

Deirdre kept staring at Frankie. "We'll come in. Our discussion is over." She brushed past Caleb and went to find Hannah.

Caleb studied his friend. Frankie— street cop, wise in the ways of the streets, but Frankie—the man, finding out women were not so easy to read or get to do what they should.

Caleb tapped Frankie on the shoulder. "Come on, Franklin. Let's go find the girls and spend some time with my boys. They were very excited to hear you were coming, especially since you were coming with Miss D."

Frankie shook off his thoughts and turned. "Franklin, eh? She's got you doing that too!"

Caleb laughed as he closed the door behind Frankie. "Naw, it was Ben."

After a supper of hamburgers and hot dogs for the boys, Caleb took Deirdre outside to show her the work that was being done in their gardens. But what he really wanted was to talk to her about what was going on.

Caleb stopped and watched her. She had stooped to pick a daisy. "Deirdre, something's going on, isn't it?"

She stopped, refusing to look at him. "What would give you that idea?"

"Other than the fact that your uncle told me you confronted someone holding a switchblade, then Frankie gives me a plate number to run, you're not acting yourself. Where would you like me to stop?"

"Caleb, you've been a cop for too long. As far as I know nothing is going on. What Ben said, it's part and parcel of the youth centre. As for now, I'm heading for home for a bit. Dad's heading overseas to the area where the cyclone went through."

She went to go past him, but stopped as he laid a hand on her arm. He waited. He knew from experience it took a while for her to respond, especially if she felt crowded or threatened.

She finally sighed and said, "I have no idea what's going on. I have had a feeling like I'm being watched but don't see anyone. There have been a couple of men looking for my hours at the centre. No one gets them. Even the staff never know when I'm going to be there, other than for the times when I have classes with the girls. That's what the staff is for—to do the day-to-day stuff." She looked up at him. "I really don't know, and I'm scared. It feels different this time. Frankie wants to stay close and I don't know if I can handle that again, if anything happens to him."

Caleb's eyes studied her, compassion filling them. She had become like a sister to him; her uncle and he were close. He reached out and pulled her into a hug.

"I know, Miss D, I know. We're praying for you. And keep Frankie close. He's got instincts that I wish I had. Let him in. He may be who God has chosen for you."

She hugged Caleb and then turned away from the house. "I need some space."

He watched with a heavy heart as she walked to the end of the yard and sat down in the swing Hannah kept there. There were things going on that no one knew about. He raised his eyes and scanned the area. He too could feel it, the eyes and the danger. He could almost smell it.

Hannah watched as he entered and sat at the table. She set a cup of tea in front of him and refilled Frankie's coffee cup.

"Is she okay?"

Caleb shrugged. "She's hurting in a way I haven't seen in years. Not since Finn."

Hannah nodded. Frankie's eyes flew between the husband and wife, who were communicating in a way he couldn't understand.

Hannah dropped a kiss on her husband's head and headed for the door.

"She wants to be alone, favourite girl," Caleb said.

"I know. She will be. I'm just going out to share a swing with a friend. No words are needed." The door clicked quietly behind her.

Caleb sighed, then picked up his cup of tea. "It's not easy loving them, Frankie, it's not easy. They have a depth to them that we can't understand."

Frankie's eyes didn't rise from his hands

Caleb looked at him, a humorous glint in his eye. "Not biting, I see." He laughed. "All right. I'll let it slide for now. But something is on your mind. Give."

Frankie nodded. "When I went to pick Deirdre up, she had been on the phone with her Dad. He said something about her not being able to go to the area where the cyclone had it. Then he called back. She had me answer. He doesn't know me, but he was very open." Frankie went on to explain what had been said to him. "So how does he know he can trust me?"

Caleb sought for the right words. "There are times when we don't and can't understand why people enter our lives. If we have been open to God, He shows us those we need at a particular time. You're it for Deirdre. Whether it's just for this, or as I suspect, you wish for more, God does this. Be there for her. Respect her Dad's wishes. Protect her. She'll fight you and fight you mightily. I can already see that's happening. She doesn't like to be put in a box and set behind a locked door. You're in the middle of a mighty powerful storm. Deirdre has been there. Talk to her." Caleb paused. "I'll need to follow up with what Brett has told you. And wait for Hannah to come up with a name."

Frankie nodded. "I figured you would." He glanced at the door. "I was doing some research on the youth centre and found a disturbing article."

Caleb waited. Frankie didn't go on with his words. Caleb sighed. "Ask her.

It's her story and she needs to be the one to clarify it with you. There's a lot more to it than what that brief article has said."

He stood and walked to the door. "It doesn't look as if the ladies are coming in any time soon. Come on, I have something to show you."

Chapter 5

Frankie pulled his truck to a stop in the driveway. Deirdre had been quiet on the drive. His attention had been on the traffic surrounding them, watchful. Given what Brett Johnson had told him, he had not relaxed his guard. He knew Caleb would be looking for anything, likely calling Eddie in to help. Ben wouldn't be asked, Caleb feeling he was too close.

He looked over at Deirdre. She was staring at the house, making no effort to get out.

"Deirdre." She didn't respond. "Deirdre, we're here. You want to get out, or would you like me to drive around for a while longer?"

She shook her head and then looked at him. "It's okay, Frankie. You don't have to. It's always so hard to come here. Just too many memories of things that went wrong."

Frankie waited.

She sighed, then looked down at her hands. "I should tell you before we go in, and it's just so hard." She stopped, then swiped at the tears on her cheeks. "I know you have probably been searching for answers. I would have if it had been me." She turned pain-filled eyes to him. "Yet you have said nothing. Why?"

He reached for her hand and clasped it in his rough scarred hand. He rubbed his thumb along the scar on the back of hers. "It's your story. You needed to tell me when you were ready. Both Ben and Caleb told me you had a story and that you would tell me. That's all they said, other than Caleb warned there was more to it than what the newspaper articles said."

She thought about that. "I have some very good friends. They are right. There's a lot more to the story than what was written." She looked at the door. "Let's go find some coffee somewhere. Dad and Mom aren't expecting us yet."

He shook his head. "No, first you need to go see your parents. Then we can talk. I'll make us some coffee, we can sit in the dim light in the house or under the moon and stars outside. Your choice." He got out and came around opening her door. "Come on, darling one. Let's get you inside."

She stepped down and then surprising him, wrapped him in a hug. "Thank you."

He reached for their bags and her briefcase, than catching her hand, led her to the door. It was unlocked. She pushed it open and told him softly to set the bags to the side of the hall.

She wandered through the house, looking for her parents. All was quiet. She guessed they had gone to bed. She sent Frankie to the kitchen, telling him where to find the coffee. She grabbed her bags and headed up the stairs. Her mother was just coming down the hall. They hugged, spoke for a minute, and then Beth headed back to bed. Deirdre dropped her bags in her room, then stood, drawing in a deep breath. This would be hard. There were things not even her parents knew about what happened. Here and now, she was ready to share with Frankie. She prayed for the words and wisdom, then headed back down the stairs.

She found Frankie standing, coffee mug in hand, looking out the large window over the sink. She grabbed her favourite mug and filled it. She looked at the window, then at Frankie.

"Inside or outside?"

He turned, watching her. "It's not cold out. Come, let's go out. Your parents have a really nice deck and furniture."

She nodded. Once on the deck she headed for a chair but a hand on her arm stopped her.

Frankie draped his arm across her shoulders and led her to the love seat. "Here. I want to sit with you beside me. I won't let you put space between us."

She studied him, then nodded. Okay, so what was really going on, she thought. She really didn't know what to think.

They sat for a while, drinking their coffee and just enjoying the sounds of the night.

Finally, Deirdre reached forward and set her mug down. She ran her hands down her jeans, hesitant to start. Frankie let his arm rest along the back of the seat, just touching her shoulders.

She spoke, "I was married, Frankie, married at 19 and widowed the same day." His hand dropped to her shoulder and rested there.

"Tell me about him." His voice was soft, hiding the emotions that were within him.

"At the time, I thought he was wonderful, the love of my life. He worked for our mission. He had been overseas and came home, surprised me when he asked. We had been dating and had briefly talked about getting married. Mom was not happy. Dad was not either but he agreed. We didn't do the whole bit, the large wedding, the large reception. I didn't even want a wedding dress. Mom and Dad were really disappointed. Looking back I guess I should have suspected something. Too young and naive." She stopped and swallowed. "This is the really hard part."

Brett stood in the kitchen. He had come down, knowing his daughter was home. Beth said she hadn't headed to bed yet. He wasn't meaning to eavesdrop but the voices carried softly over the night air. He knew he should just walk away but he needed to know what she was saying, how much she really knew. When his daughter began to speak again, he listened until he had heard what he needed to hear.

"We were supposed to fly out that night. Finn was heading back to an area where we were setting up training for disasters. He wasn't scheduled to be back for two months and surprised us all when he came back. There was something different about him. If I hadn't been so blinded at the prospect of being married, maybe I would have probed further. He wouldn't say what was wrong." She stopped, swallowed, then continued, "We had arrived at the hotel. We were heading into the hotel, then there was a drive by shooting, at least that's the official word. It wasn't. Finn had been targeted. I had no idea why, then or now. Two other people died that day. Finn had seen something and shoved me away from him. I got to walk away but my newly married husband lay dead on the pavement."

Frankie's arm came around her and pulled her close. She buried her head in his chest, tears soaking into his shirt. "The police didn't think it was a random act but they couldn't prove it. The men who did the shooting disappeared. Families were left to mourn."

Frankie's chin rested on her head as he hugged her. He couldn't speak. No wonder he had been told the story wasn't pretty.

"Did they ever find them?"

She shook her head. "No. They tried and couldn't. They suspected that they were from overseas and had headed out again as soon as they had done what they had to do." She stopped. "That's why I feel like I am being watched. I think they want what Finn gave me. He gave me nothing. I have gone through his stuff, what I have left, and have nothing."

Frankie thought about it. "Let me take a look when we go home. Maybe I can find something. Being on the streets, you learn how to hide things so they aren't found."

She pushed away from him and stood. "Sure." She watched him. "Come on. Enough gloom for the night. I"ll show you the guest room. It's just off the kitchen. Morning will be here soon enough and we always go to the early service."

"Like how early?"

"It's at 9:30. You'll love it."

Frankie groaned and then followed her in, watching as she locked the door. With a quick good night, she was gone. His sleep that night would be troubled, he knew from experience. He would get what sleep he could and be ready to protect this lady. No one had to ask him. It would get done.

****

The Watcher stood in the darkness of the trees across the street. He had had a feeling they would come here when he heard about the cyclone, and he was right. Now it was a waiting game. His experience here had taught him that she would be almost impossible to reach, surrounded by her family. He could wait but he couldn't wait long.

Chapter 6

Frankie heard voices in the kitchen the next morning as he awoke. After dressing, he stopped, then dropped back to his bed. He needed time with God this morning. He felt like he was in the middle of a tornado and he had no idea where it would drop him off.

As he opened his door, he heard laughter, then voices again.

"Don't tell me. You didn't, did you?" He heard the dismay in Deirdre's voice.

"Sure. Greg asked me the next time you were in town if we would. I told him yes."

"Timothy!" Frankie could hear the frustration in her voice. "I told him no more. I wasn't going to!"

Frankie arrived in the doorway in time to see a young man, around their age, shrug. He caught the resemblance to Ben and wondered if this was his son. His eyes went to Deirdre and he started to laugh, then struggled to keep it off his face.

Timothy shrugged. "What was I to say? You know they like to hear your voice."

"Timothy!" A wet rag was launched at him and caught him in the face.

He howled with pretended rage and went to throw it back at her, then stopped, and stuck his hand behind his back.

Frankie's head turned as he watched the woman who stood in the other doorway. This had to be Deirdre's mother but he saw no resemblance to Deirdre.

"Okay Timothy, what did you do this time?"

"Me? Nothing."

Beth waited until he shrugged, then admitted he had promised that he and Deirdre would sing the next time she was in town.

Beth shook her heard. "That's not a good promise to make. Deirdre has the right to decide if and when she wants to. This is not the right time for that, this trip." Then she turned to Deirdre. "And you, stop picking on the boys."

A howl of outrage came from Deirdre. "He started it."

Beth started laughing. "You two will never grow up. Timothy, you will need to talk to Greg and let him know she can't this time. Deirdre, you have company standing behind you. Perhaps if you stop fighting with your cousin, you could introduce us."

Deirdre's face went into her hands. "He really isn't, is he?"

This sent her mother and cousin into fresh gales of laugher. Frankie just stood there, a delighted grin on his face. This was a new side to Deirdre that he hadn't seen. He rather liked it.

Without turning, Deirdre waved a hand at her mother. "This is my mother, Beth, Franklin. That brat over there is my cousin, Timothy. Benny doesn't acknowledge he's related to him when Timothy acts like this."

At her mother's shocked voiced "Deirdre", Frankie started to laugh and came into the room.

"It's okay, really it is. I've seen her deal with the youth at the centre. I would say, Timothy, you got off very lightly."

Deirdre swatted him as he walked by him. He just laughed and took the mug of coffee he was handed. He was seeing a whole different side to her. He loved it.

Frankie settled himself into the pew. He looked around. It was an older church, pews instead of chairs, beautiful stained glass windows. Deirdre had dropped her stuff by him and then left. She returned shortly and sat beside him. Timothy had dropped down to the pew on his other side, and Beth and Brett were on Deirdre's other side.

He listened to the hymns, not the worship songs he was used to. This was different. He tilted his head to listen. He could see why Timothy and Deirdre would be asked to sing. Their voices blended in a magical way. He could listen all day.

"We'll be looking at Psalms 107:29 in particular this morning: He calmed the raging storm, and the waves became quiet. First let us look at the storm on Galilee. The storm raged, the men were frightened, the Christ was sleeping. How would you have felt? Think about that." The minister, Greg Frankie thought it was, went on to talk about that storm and the way it was calmed.

"My friends, we all face storms, whether of our own making or not. The same Christ who calmed that storm will calm yours." As Greg went on, Frankie felt Deirdre shiver. His arm went around her and he drew her close. Brett, sensing movement, peeked over his wife's head, took a look, sought out Frankie's eyes, and then frowned.

Frankie stood at the end of the service, Deirdre beside him. He looked around. He didn't know the people, but he felt the evil presence near him. Who was it and why?

Deirdre looked around. She felt uncomfortable here today, as if she was out in the middle of an open field with no shelter. She tugged at Frankie's hand and when he looked at her, she pointed to a side door. They excused themselves and they walked out.

"What's up, Deirdre?"

"I don't know. I just don't know. Something's happening here and I don't know what."

Frankie scanned the area and then headed for his truck. "We need to get you out of the open." As they walked across the street, Frankie's head shot around at the sound of an engine revving. Scooping Deirdre up, he ran for the side of the street and safety just before a gray car sped by.

He set her on her feet and hugged her, her arms tight around him.

"Tell me that really didn't happen, please."

"Sorry, darling, but it did. Someone is really after you and they have followed up here." Frankie looked around and then saw Brett watching from the other side of the street. He lifted his hand and Brett nodded. Good, he thought, he knows something is going on.

"I think we need to head back to your home and go through Finn's stuff. There has to be something there."

She sighed. "I know. I just want to help out here."

"I think your Dad will say no and send you away. I'm not sure where you will be safest."

She shook her head. "I don't think I will be safe anywhere." She stepped back, resigned as to what was needing to be done. "Let's go break the news to Mom and Dad. This is why I don't come often. I feel like I am bringing trouble to their door."

"And it has been how long?"

She shrugged. "Eight years, I don't know, ten maybe?"

"Oh, honey, no wonder." His words stopped, and she turned puzzled eyes on him.

As Frankie expected, her mother didn't it take it well, but there was something there that was different. It wasn't that she was going home instead of staying. She just couldn't define what it was. Brett just nodded. He had a good idea that something had happened that morning that was sending them home.

"Call me when you get home, Frankie." Brett had pulled Frankie aside. "Tell me what you can."

Frankie studied the older man, then nodded. "I will. Some of it has to come from Deirdre. She has never told you the full story, I don't think."

Brett sighed, then said, "No, she hasn't. I did some investigating at the time but came up empty. I never felt comfortable with the official version."

"I wouldn't have either."

****

The Watcher let some traffic pass, then pulled into the lane behind them. Good. He had them on the run. That's when mistakes would happen and he would finally get the information he needed. It had been way too long.

****

Frankie pulled off into a restaurant parking lot and turned off his truck. He scanned the area, then spoke.

"We need to eat." When she didn't speak, he reached out and touched her face. "Deirdre. I know we're on the outskirts of town, but we need to eat. We need to talk. You haven't talked to me all the way back."

She shook her head. "I don't know, Frankie. I just don't know." She reached for her door, and he stopped her. He shook his head.

"Wait, let me come around. From now on, you don't go anywhere on your own." As she started to protest, he continued, "No, whoever is after you is getting bolder. Time has to be getting short for them. So for now, consider that you have a boyfriend. That would be me." Her eyes shot to his, and he smiled. "Yes, me. We'll figure it out as we go." He paused. "We'll need to watch you at the centre. We both need to be there but we'll have to talk to Caleb, see what he can come up with." As she shook her head, he said, "Either Caleb or Ben. I think you would prefer Caleb."

Her eyes slid shut and she nodded. "Anyone but Ben. I love my uncle, but I really don't need to be smothered so much. It's bad enough now. I sometimes think he knows more than what he's saying"

Frankie studied her and then his eyes shifted to the vehicles around them. "I am sure he does. Caleb certainly seems to. If he does, Ben does. And more than likely Eddie."

She hesitated and then spoke, "Thank you, Frankie. You have never pushed. I need that."

He came around the truck and then taking her hand walked towards the restaurant. He felt like he had a target on his back and the hair on his neck bristled. Scanning the area, he kept his body between Deirdre and the driving area. He didn't want to risk another incident like this morning.

Neither had much of an appetite and they were soon walking back to Frankie's truck. Hand clasped tight in Frankie's, Deirdre moved as close to him as she could get. She felt safe with him but there was something in the air. It was getting dark, and she just wanted to be home, locked in her house and safe. But even there, she didn't feel safe.

Frankie stopped as a dark form stepped around from his truck. He started to tuck Deirdre behind him when he felt a blow between the shoulder blades and he was propelled forward into his truck and then held there. He could feel the prick of a knife at his neck.

Deirdre caught back a scream. Screaming would do no good. The patrons of the restaurant could not help and by the time help got there it might be too late.

The form came from around the truck and stopped in front of her.

"Where is it?" A guttural voice sounded, in it a tone that sent shudders through her.

"I don't know what you want." She tried to get a look at him but he was in the shadows and she couldn't see him well enough to identify him. "I don't have anything you want."

A rough hand reached out and caught her arm, the fingers squeezing together in a tight band that hurt. "Yes, you do. That husband of yours had it and gave it to you."

Deirdre kept shaking her head. "No, he didn't. He didn't give me anything. I would have known if he had."

Frankie tried to turn to watch her, but the knife dug deeper. He could feel the trickle of blood starting.

A muttered word in another language, and one at Frankie's back stepped back a bit. The knife loosened and he could breath a bit better. He was able to turn to watch Deirdre.

She was calm, steady. No fear radiated from her, but he knew she had to be afraid. He watched the two men, looking for an opportunity to down them and get Deirdre away.

The conversation continued between them. The one near Deirdre watched her, then his eyes lifted to the traffic around them. He turned and studied the vehicles. A word to his companion, and Frankie was forced to move away from his truck. Deirdre was roughly shoved after him. He reached for her hand and her fingers clung to his. They were then forced into an SUV, Deirdre in the front seat, Frankie behind the driver. There was no chance they could get away.

Frankie watched the area they were traveling through. He knew it and knew it led to a wilderness area. He didn't like this at all. He turned to watch Deirdre. Her face was still calm. How she could be so calm, he didn't know. He felt panic rising within him. Then he stopped. He was not alone. God was there in this storm. He had control. Frankie sat back, attempting to relax and plan. God knew and God would provide a way.

Chapter 7

Ben was worried. He paced around the outside of Deirdre's house. She wasn't home. Brett had called, letting him know they were on their way and to watch out for them. He hadn't said much as he was already at the airport heading away from the country.

Ben then turned to the study the house. It looked okay, windows and doors seemed intact. He pulled out his keys and searched for the one for Deirdre's front door. He hoped she was really inside and had not heard the doorbell, but he had that feeling in his gut that said otherwise. He opened the door, stepped in and turned off the alarm. He then paced through searching. She wasn't there and her briefcase that she always keep by her desk in her office was missing.

His heart sank. That meant they weren't home.

His phone rang. It was Eddie, another senior officer and close friend. Ben had called him to go check on Frankie.

"Ben, no sign of Frankie. His truck's not here and his house is still locked up solid. His neighbour said he hadn't been home since yesterday afternoon. She saw him leave and hasn't seen him again."

"That's what I was afraid of. Deirdre's not here either." He thought for a minute. "Call Caleb. He'll need to know. I have a feeling there is more involved than just a stop for a meal. Brett, Deirdre's dad, called as he was running to catch his flight. Sounds like there's been a threat come through to the office on her. He was going to have Timothy forward it to me." Ben stopped and stared around the kitchen. Nothing was moved, but it felt off, like someone had been through. "Eddie, something just doesn't feel right in the house. I can't pinpoint what. Deirdre is very particular with her stuff. It looks okay but I have that feeling."

Eddie's voice came through the phone. "I know. I do too. Frankie's too wise a street cop to get caught out. But then again, he's a man in love and that changes things." Eddie then spoke again. "I'll have Katie and Mike come out and take a look around.

They'll come in as friends, but let them in through the garage. That will hide what's happening."

Ben's voice was amused as he responded, "A man in love, eh? Yeah, I guess you could say that. Deirdre's fighting back against that." His voice sobered. "I just wish I knew where they were. I don't like this."

Eddie's voice came back through. "Where's your faith, Ben? Aren't you always telling me God's in control? He is in this. No matter what happens."

Ben shuddered at the thought. "I know, Eddie, I know. Tell Caleb to call me."

****

The Watcher turned and looked around. He didn't know who that was who entered her house. He hoped that he would not find the information. He would need to be stopped. He knew his men had found the two and had them with them. This was up to him. He stepped quietly through the yard, up the steps and to the door. It swung silently open and he stopped and waited. He stepped in and waited. He could hear movement in the house, and he crept towards it. He stopped once more, barely moving. He stepped forward again and as the man's body turned towards him, he struck. The man went down with just a whisper of a sound. The Watcher looked around and then crept back out. He would stand and watch and wait. His men would soon let him know where they were.

****

Eddie met Caleb on the sidewalk leading to Frankie's house.

Caleb looked at the house, then around the neighbourhood. "I just wish this would stop. We've had too many in the last year.:

Eddie nodded. "I know. It's going to hit the men hard. He's one of us." He turned to face the house. "We'll have no end of volunteers to search. If they have been taken for whatever reason, those involved will wish they hadn't. Deirdre is one of us too. She's Ben niece, but she's Frankie's girl."

"Has it gone that far?"

"Not officially, but I know Frankie. In his mind, she's his. She'll take longer to make that decision."

"I think she already has. She's just too afraid of what happened in the past to expect to have happiness with someone else. Come on, let's go search his house. I doubt we'll find much but at least we'll know."

Caleb's phone rang as they were walking through the downstairs. As the voice at the other end spoke, his eyes closed and then he grabbed for Eddie's arm. Pulling him with him, he locked up Frankie's house.

"What's up?"

"Ben. Katie and Mike found him down in the house. Katie's on her way to get Marg. Mike has called in for more men to come help him."

"Did she say how bad?"

Caleb shook his head. "I'll meet you there. Once we know what's going on, I'll want you at Deirdre's."

Frankie watched as the SUV stopped in front of a house. It was isolated but he could see lights not that far away. He scouted around the area with his eyes, taking in what he could in the dim light. Trees were close but the underbrush was cleared. There were a couple of outbuildings and he thought he saw light reflect off another vehicle. His heart sank. How were they to get out?

The doors opened and they were pulled from the vehicle and then shoved towards one of the outbuildings. It was unlocked and they were pushed inside. The door swung shut and he heard the lock click. He stood and stared around. There were a couple of windows and the door. The floor was dirt, he could feel the cold and dampness through his feet.

He heard Deirdre moving around the building. When she stopped in front of one of the windows, he went towards her. Her posture was stiff and he could feel the anger vibrating within her. His hand went to her shoulder.

"I am very ticked off right now, Franklin."

"Just ticked off? I'm just a touch mad myself."

Her elbow caught him in the ribs. "You know what I mean. I could be really angry but that solves nothing." She turned slightly. "How's the neck?"

"It's okay, just a little prick."

"It looked a whole lot worse than a little prick."

He felt it. It was tiny and when he got out of here, he would have it looked at if he needed to.

"So what's your plan?" Deidre asked as she continued to move around the room.

"I have no idea as yet. Do you have one?"

"Of course." He stopped and stared at her. "Of course, I do. I've been in lots worse situations and with much meaner men. Follow me and I'll get you out."

Frankie shook his head and then turned her to face him. Standing with his hands on her shoulders, he spoke, "Deirdre. Please. Don't do anything foolish."

She shrugged off his hands. "I'm getting out of here and out of here tonight. You can come or stay, whichever you want."

He watched as she dug down in her pocket and pulled out something. She showed him what looked like a knife but then she headed for the door. Inserting it into the lock, she wiggled it and then he heard a click.

"Is that legal here? I highly doubt it. And I don't even want to know where you got it. Well, maybe I should find out, if it was here in our country."

"Probably not, but it looks like a pocket knife, so I can get away with it. No one but you knows what it really does. And no, I didn't get it here." She pushed the door open and looked around. "Come on, we can get out of here now."

He crept through the door behind her and she closed and locked it after them. Then he watched in amazement as she headed for the SUV. A few minutes later, she was once again by his side. She stopped at the second vehicle and then she led him towards the woods.

"Deirdre, what did you do?"

"Something my beloved cousin taught me. I let the air out of all their tires and took the tire valve caps." She grabbed his hand and dropped something in it. Sure enough, that's what was in his hand.

Frankie laughed softly. "I still wouldn't want to meet you in a dark alley. You're too scary." He looked behind him. "I just wish I knew if we had time to get away."

"We do. They're planning on leaving us there overnight and then questioning us in the morning. Whoever hired them will be here some time tomorrow morning. We have time as long as we move quickly."

"How do you know that? They were speaking another language."

She shrugged. "I pick up languages very easily. Give me a month in a country and I speak like a native. It's a gift but can also be a curse. Come now, we need to get moving. And yes, before you ask, I have been in that country long enough to pick up the language."

Frankie stopped her. "Did they take your phone?"

She smirked. "No and I bet they didn't take yours either. They certainly aren't from here. That's the first thing they should have done."

He pulled out his phone as they walked forward. "No service here. Let's go."

"Can you hotwire a car?"

He stopped and stared at her. "Hotwire a car? Really? And I suppose you can?"

She nodded and he just stared at her, mouth open. "Of course, I can. But you didn't say if you could if we found one."

He shook his head, grabbed her hand and pulled her with him. "I tell you. You're very scary. I must remember not to get on your bad side. And yes, I can hotwire a car. Now who taught you? Timothy?"

He felt her head shake and he stopped once again to stare at him. "Who then?"

"Well, I guess you could say Raffaele, then Pietro, then Thomas."

He held up his hand and she giggled. "Enough. I gather these are all men from your adventures?"

"No, just boys, usually under the age of 10."

He shook his head and then started forward again. "You're scary. Your friends are scary. I'm never going to be safe around you or them. No one will be safe around you."

Her laugh warmed his heart even as he feared they never make it out of the trees alive.

Chapter 8

Marg met Caleb at the Emergency Department door.

"How is he?" He could tell she was frightened for her husband but her demeanour was calm.

"He's awake. The Emergency doctor is with him right at the moment. I'll take you back soon."

"What happened, Caleb? He said he was worried about Deirdre and left. Then Katie called and came to get me."

"He was at Deirdre's, found something I gather and then had called for Katie and Mike to come over. He was attacked while waiting for them. He doesn't remember much other than being in her kitchen and then waking up here."

Marg's eyes slid shut. "Thank you, God. I was so scared."

Caleb nodded and then turned. "Come on. I'll take you back. The doctor said he could go home tonight."

Caleb watched as his friend held his hand out to his wife, then he turned and walked away. He was headed for Deirdre's house. Maybe they had come up with something.

Eddie met him in the living room.

"Nothing. Absolutely nothing."

Caleb looked around and drew a deep breath. "No sign of either one of them, I gather."

"No, and they're not answering their phones." Eddie looked around. "I have had enough of this. Three was plenty and now we're into four."

Caleb smiled and nodded. "I know. Our friends just seem to be attracting trouble."

"If it's in the water, I'm giving that up. I'll drink juice instead."

Caleb laughed at Eddie's grumbling. "No, it might be in the air, and you can't stop breathing that."

Eddie glared at him, then laughed. "I know, you're right. I just wish I knew why."

"So do I, Eddie. Katie and Mike are finished?"

"They are. They didn't find anything though. If the place was searched, it was done by an expert who took ample precautions." Eddie shook his head. "I just don't get it."

"Me neither, Eddie. Ben's fine. Marg was there to take him home."

"Did he remember anything?"

"No. He's angry. And worried. He said he would be calling Beth tonight."

"Will Brett come home?"

Caleb thought about that. "I really don't know, Eddie. I really don't know." He hesitated, choosing his words. "I never liked how Deirdre was left on her own all those years ago. She ran, but they let her."

"Did they ever figure out if Finn was the target or one of the other men?"

Caleb turned to stare at Eddie. "Now that's an idea of where to look. Find out everything you can on Finn. There was just something that has never satisfied me with that."

"That I can do, Caleb. If you can get me the country he came back from, I may have a friend over there who can search out information there."

Caleb nodded. "That I can do."

"Meanwhile, it's not that late. I'm going to take a drive around the area of town where they would have come back through. Maybe I'll find something."

Caleb watched Eddie walk away. He was burdened for his friends in a way that he had not been in a long time. What storm, Lord, he asked, what storm is gathering, ready to hit our town and my friends?

****

The Watcher stood in his house and looked around. Finally, he had her where he wanted her. She would tell him where to find the information he was looking for. But first, a celebratory dinner was being prepared for him. A good night's sleep and he would head out to where she was being held. The man with her was not important.

His minions would dispose of him without a second thought.

****

Frankie stopped and looked around. His sense of direction was keen and he knew now where they were. Just ahead would be the parking lot they had been abducted from.

"Isn't that where this all started?" Deirdre's voice was quiet beside him.

"It is. We need to wait, though. I don't want to rush to my truck just in case they did find out we're gone."

She shook her head. "Trust me. They won't. In their country, a locked door stops people. They don't break out and run."

"No, it's only scary people like you who do."

She shoved him and then pointed. "Look, someone has stopped near your truck."

Frankie peered through the darkness and then grabbing her hand, pulled her closer to the truck. "I think that's Eddie."

"Eddie?"

He nodded. "Eddie. I've trusted him with my life before. If we could only get his attention somehow."

Deirdre looked around. "I can."

Frankie shook his head and looked at her. "No."

She slipped her hand from his and was gone before he could stop her. He watched as she changed her gait and seemed to shrink. This girl's good, he thought. She really would survive on the streets. I think she's even better than Ashling, Liam's wife.

Eddie tried the doors on Frankie's truck. Locked. He cupped his hands and peered inside but it was too dark to see much. He turned as a woman approached him.

"Can I help you, ma'am?"

She mumbled some words and Eddie stepped closer.

"It's Deirdre. Frankie's behind me somewhere. Here's his keys. Grab our stuff as if you were sent for it, then leave and park at the gas station two blocks down. We'll find you." Deirdre limped her way past him towards the restaurant, as if that had been her goal all the time.

Eddie turned to watch, then looked down at his hands. Sure enough, he had keys in his hands.

Frankie watched in amazement as Eddie unlocked his truck and pulled both their bags and the briefcase out, locked the vehicle again, and then headed for his car to leave. He felt his pockets. She really had picked his pocket for his keys. He was almost afraid to think of what she would do next.

He felt her come up beside him and waited.

"Eddie's meeting us down the block at the gas station. We need to move now."

Frankie's hand went out and stopped her. "When did you pick my pocket?"

He caught a flash of a grin and a shake of her head. "You never felt a thing, did you? I did about ten minutes ago."

Frankie stared at her, shook his head and then caught her hand. "Come on, let's go home. And I want to know what other skills you have that you haven't shared with me."

"I have plenty. When you get caught in trouble overseas, you learn quickly to adapt and figure out how to survive. These are survival skills I've had to learn."

"That's it." Frankie declared. "I'm never letting you go overseas again. At least, not without me."

Eddie eyed the two as they shut the doors of his car behind them. "Are you both all right?" At their nod, he pulled away from the station and headed back into town. "Caleb is going to want to see you. I'm taking you there."

His eyes searched Deirdre's face in the rearview mirror. She was tired and dirty, more than likely hungry, he thought.

"Deirdre, Ben went to your house to look for you. He thought someone had been through it and called in one of our teams. While he was waiting, he was attacked." At her gasp, he continued, "He's fine, other than a headache. Marg was taking him home. He didn't see who it was though." His eyes questioned her silently.

She shook her head in denial. "I don't know, Eddie, I don't know who it would have been."

He nodded. He pulled into Caleb's driveway, turned off the ignition, and then turned to them.

"This situation is escalating. We need to figure out who. The why is easy. Someone wants something you have. It has to be something of Finn's."

Deirdre's eyes slid shut as she nodded. "I know. I don't have anything of his left. I never had much of his anyway, just some books and a few trinkets. We were too young to have gathered much."

"There has to be something we're missing. We'll keep you safe and figure it out in the meantime."

Caleb met them at the door, scanning their faces. He felt relief wash through him that they were okay.

"Come on back to the kitchen. Hannah has some soup and sandwiches ready. We hadn't eaten earlier. The boys ate and she put them to bed."

Hannah gave Deirdre a look and then turned to Caleb. "They're cleaning up first before eating and being questioned."

Deirdre shot a surprised look at Caleb, caught his small smile at his wife, and then felt better knowing he wasn't angry. She followed Hannah up the stairs to a guest room.

"There's a shower in there and I'll find you some clean clothes."

"Actually Hannah, if one of them could grab my bag from Eddie's car, I have clean clothes."

Hannah nodded and headed back down the stairs.

Fifteen minutes later, feeling much cleaner and more like herself, she opened the door to the room and stepped outside. Frankie was leaning on the wall across from the door, waiting for her. He had had a chance to clean up as well. He looked at her, then opened his arms and she walked into them. He hugged her tight, without saying a word, then turned her to walk down the stairs. They needed food first. Then the questioning would begin. He was really looking forward to seeing the looks of Caleb's and Eddie's faces when he told them how they had got away. It would be priceless.

Hannah set soup and sandwiches before them, then seated herself at the table.

Caleb went to ask something, then caught his wife's eye. He smiled and nodded. Yes, he could and would wait.

When the two finally pushed away their bowls and plates, Caleb looked around the table. Now would come the hard part, trying to figure out who and why. And Hannah had not yet given him a name.

"Who wants to start?" He eyed Frankie and Deirdre.

They looked at each other. Frankie's eyes grew big as Deirdre started to laugh.

"You don't know this lady, Caleb. She's scary. She's got scary friends. Don't meet her in a dark alley." He shuddered dramatically.

"Behave yourself. It wasn't that bad, not as bad as you're making out."

Frankie nodded his head. "Oh, yes, it was. You are very scary."

By this time, the eyes of the other three were bobbing between the two. Caleb finally held up a hand.

"Please, guys. I would really like to know why Frankie thinks you're so scary, Deirdre."

This sent Deirdre off into fresh gales of laughter.

Frankie looked at Caleb and shook his head in a sorrowful manner. "She is scary, Caleb. I could have used her on the streets. There wouldn't have been a speck of trouble." By this time, Deirdre had pillowed her head on her arms on the table, shoulders shaking.

Eddie was starting to smile. Having dealt with her and Frankie's truck, he wasn't going to be surprised with what was coming, he knew.

Hannah watched the two closely, sensing there was more going on that what showed on the surface. She was glad. These two were just so right for one another.

"Frankie."

"Okay, Caleb, but don't say I didn't warn you that she's scary. She takes switchblades off teenagers without much of a protest. She carries a knife, or what she says is a pocket knife, but she can pick locks with it and then lock it again as if it had never opened. She blames her cousin for teaching her how to disable a car. She actually removed all the tire valve caps from two SUVs. Two, not just one! She can hotwire a car and says it was kids that taught her. She can pick a pocket and no one even knows. She's scary. Her friends are scary."

By this time, Frankie's narrative had the other three in laughter.

When he was finally able to talk, Caleb turned to Deirdre. "Scary, eh? Did you really do all that?"

She nodded, her eyes sparkling with mirth. "All except hotwire a car. We didn't need to."

"I forgot." Frankie spoke up. "She can even learn a language in a month."

They turned to stare at her and she shrugged. "It happens. Now, about today.

We had headed home, stopped for something to eat, and then when we were walking back to Frankie's truck, we were stopped. Frankie needs to get his neck checked out. One of the men held a knife to him and I know it cut into the flesh. We were taken to a house about an hour away, middle of the woods. They locked us in an outbuilding and then disappeared. Their conversation went along the lines of 'We'll leave them here, he'll be out tomorrow morning, we'll question them then, they can't get out of here.' Well, locks don't hold me in. Stop laughing, Frankie. As Frankie said, I picked the lock, got us out, locked the door so they wouldn't know until they unlocked it, stole the tire valve caps (they won't be going anywhere any time soon), and walked back to the restaurant. I walked up to Eddie, gave him Frankie's keys, he got our stuff, met us at a gas station, and here we are."

Caleb and Eddie were staring at her, mouths open. Hannah had laid her hand on Deirdre's arm and was watching Frankie. Frankie was sitting there, shaking his head, still somewhat in disbelief. Yes, she thought, Deirdre is so good for Frankie. He is coming alive and losing that beat-up look he had had for so long. Thank you, Lord.

Caleb swallowed, and then said, "That's what really happened? You just unlocked the door and waltzed out of there?"

She smiled at Frankie and then looked at Caleb. "Just about. Except Frankie keeps saying I'm scary. I'm not. I know people who are a lot scarier."

Caleb looked at Eddie, who was staring at Deirdre.

"You know people who are scarier than you?" At her nod, Eddie looked at the ceiling. "Heaven help us if they're in this town. And does your uncle know?"

She reached over and patted his hand. "They're not. I left them overseas. And yes, he does. He helped teach me."

At that, they all broke up in laughter.

Sobering, Caleb watched her. "Someone was looking for something in your house. Do you have any idea why or what?"

She thought about that, then shook her head. "I have very little in my house. After seeing how little my friends have overseas, things aren't important to me. I have some keepsakes, mainly from my trips and gifts those friends have given me. I don't have anything of Finn's if that's what they were looking for. Come to think of it, he really didn't give me a lot or write a lot." She looked sad at that.

She looked at Caleb. "I will need to go back over the house again, I guess."

"You will, but it can wait until tomorrow. Right now, I would say you two need some sleep and I know I could use some."

Chapter 9

Timothy stood in his parents' kitchen the next morning. His aunt had sent him home. She told him he needed to be here. He wasn't as sure though.

He turned as he heard his mother enter the kitchen. She stopped, then crossed the room to hug him.

"I'm so glad you're here, Timothy. It's time you came home." She stepped back to look up at him, taking in the dark brown hair and hazel, almost brown eyes. He looked so much like his father at that age.

"I'm glad. Aunt Beth really laid it on the line. I think they are really regretting the way they handled it with Deirdre all those years ago."

Marg nodded. "I'm sure they are. They handled it very poorly. I'm just glad she came to your Dad and I."

Timothy drew in a breath. "How's Dad this morning?"

"He's got a headache but he'll be down shortly. He says he has to go in, even though Caleb told him to stay home today."

"He would." Timothy looked down at his mother. "What would you say if I told you I was moving back here, looking for something to do here?"

Marg studied her son, then smiled. "It would make your Dad and I very happy. But most importantly, it has to be what God wants you to do. Is it?"

He nodded. "I'm getting to that point. That's part of the reason I came. I want to be here for Deirdre. What do you think is going on?"

Marg sighed, then sat at the table with the cup of coffee she had been fixing. She patted the table beside her and Timothy sat with his own cup. "I don't really know, son. I think it has to do with Finn but it could be something from one of her trips. She has gone to some pretty hard areas of the world. Why would Brett even let her when he won't go to them himself?"

Timothy stared across the kitchen, not sure how to express himself. He saw his father standing quietly in the doorway, not entering so as not to disturb the conversation. "Uncle Brett has changed. I can't explain it. It's like he's going through the motions and not really focused on who goes where. Aunt Beth is different too. I just can't figure it out."

Ben entered the room, dropped a kiss on his wife's head, laid a hand on his son's shoulder, then sat at the table as well. "He has, Timothy. I have noticed that the last few times we've talked. I can't get a straight answer from him. I'm not sure if he even knows why or how."

After they had spent some time in family prayer, Ben stood and looked at his son. "I think you should go spend some time with Deirdre." As Timothy went to protest, Ben held up his hand. "I know, she has Frankie, but she needs family as well. You are probably the one closest to her. She needs us right now. Frankie does, too. He has never said much about his family, so I know if he has some, he's not close to them."

Timothy nodded. "I'll head over there, unless Mom wants some time with me."

His mother smiled. "With what you said about moving back here, I'll have plenty of time. Go, spend some time with Deirdre. Get to know Frankie. He's been beat up by his time on the streets and I suspect long before that, but he is softening. Your cousin has worked wonders in directing him back to God." Marg paused, then said softly, "And I think that's what you're looking to do, renew yourself."

"I am, Mom, I am. See you later."

Frankie stood in Deirdre's kitchen and looked around. She was right. She really didn't have a lot of what he always called stuff. She had some nice pictures, some ornaments that obviously meant something to her, and not much more.

Deirdre looked around her living room. Eddie stood watching her.

"Can't see anything obvious?" He asked.

She shook her head. "No. I really can't. Finn was overseas a lot the last year or so before we married so we never had time to collect things. We had planned on living overseas for about six months, then moving back here." She walked over to the bookshelves and pulled out a photo album. "This is the only album I have that has anything in it from that time. You're welcome to take it and look through it if you think it will help"

Eddie took it from her and briefly glanced through it. "Thanks. I'll do that, then get it back to you."

She shrugged. "No rush. That's a time in my life that has come and gone. Going back over pictures and whatnot won't bring it back."

Frankie's puzzled eyes met Eddie's over Deirdre's head. They both wondered at her words.

After a tap at the door, Timothy entered. He greeted the two men and gave his cousin a hug. "So, what are we up to today?"

"Not stealing tire valve caps, I hope." Eddie's dry tone brought on the laughter.

Timothy looked at his cousin and groaned. "Don't tell me. You really didn't, did you?"

She nodded and held up eight fingers. He shook his head. "That was a joke, Deirdre. I never ever thought you would do that."

Frankie spoke from the doorway. "If she hadn't, we may not be standing here today. Your cousin is very scary."

Timothy took a look at Frankie, then Eddie, and finally his cousin. He smiled and shook his head. "She is. Very scary."

Deirdre slapped her cousin's arm as Eddie headed for the door. "I had your truck brought back to your place, Frankie. Keys through the mail slot, but I gather you have a friend who could pick the lock and hotwire it for you." On a laugh from the men and a squeal of outrage from Deirdre, he shut the door.

Frankie looked around the living room after Eddie left, then turned his gaze on Timothy. Timothy was turning an object over and over in his fingers. "What's that?"

Timothy looked up. "I really don't know. I found it in our warehouse one night, and just never threw it way."

"Can I see it?" Frankie took it from Timothy and looked it over. It was a piece of silver, he thought, engraved. There seemed to be an edge that wasn't smooth and he needed to get a better look at that.

Deirdre had come to stand near him. At her surprised gasp, he looked at her. She was pulling a necklace from around her neck. It held a similar object. She removed it from the chain and held it out to him. He looked at both of them, examining them well.

"I need a piece of paper I can lay these down on." Timothy handed him a sheet of paper from the printer, and Frankie headed for the kitchen.

Laying the two objects on the paper, he slid them close together. He twisted them one way and another, then they clicked together. He concentrated on them and then looked up at the other two.

"This may be what they are looking for. We need to get this to Eddie or Caleb.

Timothy, it won't look strange if you go there, looking for your Dad. It would be expected that you would be meeting him for lunch or something seeing as you're in town. Deirdre and I can't be out and about much until we catch those men."

Plans were quickly devised and Timothy sent on his way. Deirdre looked at Frankie and sighed, "Now what?"

"We wait and see what that brings. In the meantime, we are going to search your house, and I mean search. Every book and picture will be looked at. There has to be something here."

****

The Watcher stood in the doorway of the outbuilding, anger and rage evident on his face. Where were they? He had been assured they were here and could not escape. The men he had hired were useless, he thought, absolutely useless. They had them in their grasp and let them escape.

"Find them and bring them to me. As long as they can talk, bring them to me. The man, I don't care about. Finish him off if you have to. Bring me that woman."

The two men looked at each other and then at him. They were dumbstruck that the two had escaped. The door was locked, windows not disturbed, no holes anywhere they could get out of.

****

Eddie tapped at Caleb's door and then entered, closing the door behind him. He sank into one of the chairs in front of Caleb's desk and sighed, tapping the folder he held.

Caleb waited, knowing Eddie would speak when the time was right. Finally, he asked, "What did you find out?"

"You're not going to like it and I am not going to like having to totally destroy a young woman's memories and life."

Caleb watched his friend. Whatever he had found out lay heavy on him.

"Which do you want to start with? I can handle the not liking it. Tell me and then we can figure out how to tell Deirdre."

Eddie opened the folder, studied the contents, then handed the closed file to Caleb. "Read this and then we'll talk."

Caleb shot him a glance as he accepted the folder. He opened it and began to read. Eddie watched the distressed look cross his friend's face and raised his heart in prayer. This was going to hurt, no matter how they approached it. Someone had been keeping some terrible secrets that would blow apart a world or two in their friends' lives.

Caleb finished reading it, then laid the folder down on his desk. His eyes slid closed. Eddie was right. This was life changing.

"Did you have any idea when you started looking?"

Eddie shook his head. "None. Whoever did the initial investigation swept it under the rug. Makes me wonder if money changed hands. I had to do some hard digging to get this much."

Caleb shook his head. "I have no idea how we are ever going to approach this with her. It was totally destroy what she has believed for years and totally change how she looks at herself."

"I wish I could get my hands on him. They have absolute proof he died in that shooting but he took two other men with him and destroyed their families as well." Eddie stopped. "I just wonder if his parents knew. Deirdre doesn't seem to talk much about them and I can't find much on them in this country in the last 10 years."

Caleb eyed him and then spoke, "I have a contact at the federal level. Let me call him. He might be able to get us more information than we can lay our hands on. Let's keep this between us until I hear back from him. This is really going to hit Ben hard."

Eddie rose and then spoke, "It will. I just don't understand her parents. I wouldn't have let a girl of mine run like that."

Caleb shook his head. "Me either, even if she is scary."

Eddie laughed. "Frankie sure knows how to play that one. She's good for him. I don't think I've ever seen him so lighthearted."

"That she is. He's also finding his way back to God. That goes a long way."

Eddie nodded. "I'll keep digging. If I find out anything more, I'll call you."

Ben stood at the door, just ready to knock as Eddie opened it. "Wait will you, Eddie? Timothy has just brought in something I think you will both to look at."

Caleb looked up as Ben and Timothy entered. Eddie shut the door again and approached the desk as Timothy laid down an envelope.

"Frankie figured this out. He saw me with one of these, realized Deirdre had one, played with them and they went together. I have no idea what they are."

Caleb opened the envelope and slid out the joined stones. He studied them.

"Ben, Eddie, any idea?"

Ben shook his head. "All I can think of is a map, but that really doesn't fit what we're seeing."

Eddie studied them closer. "I think you're on the right track, Ben. They seem to be map when together. When separate, they are really meaningless. It almost seems, though, that there should be another piece to it."

Caleb looked closer. "You could be right. Who do we have that is skilled in this? Whoever it is, get it to them and warn them I'll fire them if they even think about talking about it."

"That I will." Eddie picked up the envelope, slid the stones back in and left.

Ben and Timothy spoke with Caleb a bit longer, then Timothy left.

Ben hesitated, and Caleb watched him.

"Sit, Ben. Tell me what's up."

Ben sat and looked at his hands. "I really don't know, Caleb. I can feel something but I don't know what it is. Just this sense of impending doom."

Caleb nodded. "I know. That worries me. And no, Hannah has not given me a name yet." He paused. "It's more than that, isn't it?"

Ben nodded. "There is. Timothy is talking about moving back here and he loves working for the mission. He said Beth pushed him to come home and that's not her." He looked up at Caleb, distress in his face. "I just wish I knew what was going on. Deirdre's in trouble and now my own son is not being open with me, not like he usually is."

Caleb watched his friend. "I don't know what to say, Ben, except we'll pray and pray hard. God is still in control. He'll watch out for them." He smiled. "Besides, you have a niece who's very scary."

Ben laughed. "Who told you that? Let me guess, Frankie. He's just beginning to know that girl. She has had experiences she has never talked about and learned things you and I would never ever had thought a woman should know."

Chapter 10

The Watcher stood across the street from Deirdre's house. She was there. How she got away he couldn't understand. She had gotten out of a locked building and appeared back here as if nothing had happened. He needed to get to her but now she had two with her. He really did need what she had. Time was running out and running out quickly.

****

Frankie watched as Deirdre wandered her house, touching pictures and then objects. She just couldn't settle down.

"Deirdre." She looked at him and he patted the couch beside him. "Come, sit down. You're going to wear a hole in the floor otherwise."

She shook her head. "I can't. I'm still trying to figure out who those men were."

"No, come, sit."

She grudgingly did, crossing her arms in an angry manner. He angled his body so he could watch her.

She sighed and then uncrossed her arms. "I'm sorry. That's not a good attitude. I shouldn't take it out on you. I just want to go back to what it was last week. Being safe. Working at the youth centre. Living my life the way I want."

Frankie nodded. "I know you do, and you will." He watched emotions flickering across her face. "We'll get back there and soon. Caleb and Eddie are really good at digging."

"I know they are and so in Ben, but I don't want Ben involved. He's too close."

"What about Timothy?"

She thought about that and then looked at him. "There's something going on there. I have no idea what but for him to be here while the mission is working a crisis, that's not normal."

Frankie thought about that. "I would tend to agree with you. It's not in his character. But something had triggered him coming home and I am going out on a limb and says it's permanent. It feels like he has given up on the mission and is coming back here, not to lick his wounds but to go on with his life."

She laid her head back and then nodded. "I think you're right. He and I grew close when I came back here all those years ago. He definitely wants to talk with me but doesn't know how to approach it."

Frankie reached for her Bible on the end table. "Tell me again about those verses, the ones about calming the sea and about finding comfort and rest. You have helped me to find them. I think you need to find them yourself."

She turned her head to study him. He was right. She was growing tired in her heart and soul. She needed what resting in God would bring. She reached out her hand to him and thanked him.

Eddie tapped at Caleb's door and then entered. He sank heavily into one of the chairs.

Caleb finished his phone conversation and then looked at Eddie. His heart sank. He could tell he wasn't going to like what he would hear. A prayer rose to heaven as he waited.

"Do we need to pull Ben in?"

Eddie looked at him, then at the ceiling. "Read what I have and then decide. I'm thinking we'll have to but I'll let you make the call."

Caleb reached for the file and opened it. Eddie was right. Ben would need to be involved but it was going to really hurt.

"Your source is sure he's back here?"

Eddie nodded. "Same flight, two rows back, aisle seat opposite side. He paid dearly for that seat. He was watching her then."

"And he's in town?"

"He couldn't make the same flight she did that day. He tried hard. He flew in the next morning. He has brought two men back with him. I would suspect they're the ones who they had the run-in with. Nasty characters. If they catch up to Deirdre and Frankie again, it won't go so well. They dislike being bested but to be bested by a woman, that pretty much writes her obituary."

Caleb shuddered. "Then we'll have to make sure they stay safe. But where?"

"I know. It seems all our safe houses are known. Frankie might be safe on the streets, he has so many contacts and friends. Deirdre, she might be or she might not be. Depends on how scary she is."

Caleb shook his head. "I still can't believe what they were saying. I thought Frankie was good, but is she that much better?"

Eddie thought about that. "She has spent time in all those countries, in some pretty rough and rotten areas. It is completely possible that she has learned survival skills we would not even consider necessary here. She's quiet, doesn't say much but there's a hard layer in her that shows every once in a while. I would say that it's about to be shown. Ben has said she can put a man down without really even trying."

Caleb studied the notes and then sighed. "We're going to have to talk to them but we'll need a plan first. Otherwise, she'll run and take Frankie, or he'll run and take her. We also need to watch for Timothy. If it was found out he had one of those stones, they'll be after him too."

"It just keeps growing, doesn't it? And you're sure Hannah hasn't given you a name?"

Caleb shook his head. "Not this time. The Lord's being silent with her."

"Which one of us gets to break the news?"

Caleb smiled. "You?"

"That's what I was afraid of. I get to go talk to a scary lady."

Caleb laughed as Eddie walked away, and then sobered. Things were taking a turn and he didn't like the way they were turning. His phone rang and he was delighted to hear his wife's voice. They spoke for a few minutes, then her tone changed.

"You have a name, don't you?"

"I do, Caleb, I do. It's just going to hurt so much when it comes out."

"Tell me."

She told him and he closed his eyes. She was right. It was really going to hurt. The name she gave was the same as the one Eddie had found.

Eddie tapped at Deirdre's door. Frankie checked to see who it was and then let him in, scanning the street as he did.

Deirdre stepped in from the kitchen, drying her hands on a towel.

"You don't look very happy, Eddie."

"I have some news, and I am not sure how to tell you."

"Are my parents, Ben and Marg, and Timothy all right?" At his nod, she continued, "Then what you have to say may not be as important as you think it is."

"Oh, it is. Come, sit, Deirdre. This will take a bit."

Deirdre watched him with apprehension, then sank to the couch. Frankie sat beside her, arm on the back of the couch for support. She watched Eddie as he tried to find words.

Eddie stared at her, grief tracing his face. "I really don't know how to begin,

Deirdre.   What I have to say will dramatically change your life." He paused. "What I am about to say we have verified with more than one source.   This should have been done years ago and wasn't."

Deirdre shared a look with Frankie, then stared at Eddie. "What is it, Eddie?"

"How much do you know about what Finn was doing for the mission that last year?"

She shrugged. "Not that much, I don't think.   He never really said and I was too busy in school to ask much. Why?"

"We have discovered that Finn was involved in black market trading of relief supplies.   He was being bought off too by corrupt government officials and we suspect doing a little blackmailing on the side.

"That stone that he gave you has a clue to the information. Timothy found the second one in the mission warehouse, where Finn should never have been."   Eddie paused. The hardest part was coming, and he could already see tears in her eyes. He saw Frankie's hand come down on her shoulder.

Eddie continued, "Now this is the really hard part. I know you have always wondered who the real target was. It was Finn except they didn't want him dead. They wanted the information he had hidden on those stones. We're not sure yet if there is another one or not." He paused. "There's no easy way to say what I have to say. You didn't have much of a wedding, did you?" She shook her head. "Didn't think so. A lady like you deserves all the bells and whistles, even back then, instead of a little tiny wedding like you had. I hate to tell you what I must." Eddie paused again. "Your minister was not a minister. He was an actor Finn hired. Your wedding certificate, it's a fake. You were never married, are not a widow. He was using you to get out of this country. He had plans to leave you at the hotel once you were checked in and disappear."

Deirdre's eyes were wide with shock and her hands covered her mouth. To think that this is what Finn had brought her to. Not married. Not widowed. Living a fake life. Frankie's hand was heavy on her shoulder. What must he think, she thought? He was becoming such a part of her life.

She stood and paced the room, thoughts running rampant through her mind. All these years, to come to this? And the men from overseas? Who hired them?

"Who hired them?"

"What?"

"The men. Who hired them? Someone from here or from overseas?"

Eddie was amazed at how quickly she got to the centre of it all. "That we are still working on, but they do not come from that country. It looks, from what my contact says, that time is running out and without the information Finn had on them, they will be facing multiple charges. Whoever has hired them will be facing multiple charges as well as murder charges."

Frankie shuddered. "And they really don't care then if Deirdre dies, so long as they don't?"

Eddie shook his head. "No, they don't. We still have to identify who is in charge here but we do know he returned on the same flight as you did, Deirdre, and tried to book a flight back here on your flight."

Deirdre stopped pacing to stare at him. "So now what? I obviously can't go back to the youth centre or church. I'm not going around my parents or Ben and Marg."

"Caleb feels Timothy may be a target as well if they have found out he had one of those stones. Timothy will be tucked away somewhere safe today and no one will know where."

"So where do we go?" Frankie asked.

Deirdre spun to look at him, shaking her head. "No way. I'm on my own with this one. You're not coming."

Frankie shook his head. "Nope, you're not scaring me today. You're stuck with me. Where you are, I'll be. I need you to remind me how to ride out a storm."

Deirdre kept shaking her head.

Finally, Eddie spoke up. "Actually, Caleb does plan for the two of you to be together. Where, we'll still trying to figure out. We could always send you back to the street, Frankie. Deirdre would protect you in those dark alleyways."

Frankie snickered as Deirdre spun to confront Eddie. "Not you, too. I am not that scary."

"Hey, I'm just repeating what I've been told."

At another snicker from Frankie, Deirdre spun and narrowed her eyes at him. "No more comments from the peanut gallery."

"Seriously, you two. We need to make some plans and make them now. We know the one who is after you is in town now. He has the two thugs that nabbed you here in town. He will not hesitate to harm or even kill anyone who gets in his way. We want to tuck you away somewhere and we have to figure it out. You won't be going to the youth centre. You won't be going to church. You will be staying away from your family. There's no give or take in that. They will use any of the venues to get to you."

Deirdre shivered and then sat down beside Frankie again. "I just can't take all this in. You are absolutely sure about Finn?"

At Eddie's nod, she hid her face in her hands. "Talk about betrayal. He never really intended me to go with him, did he?"

"No, he didn't. But I don't think he ever intended to die that day. He likely thought he had time to get away and didn't realize they were so close. I don't think we'll ever completely understand his motivation."

Frankie studied the woman sitting beside him. He knew he wanted her in his life all the time. He had come to love her heart and her mind. "So, Eddie, where do we go from here?" he asked.

"Right now, we keep you here. We have officers outside and around the block. Frankie, if you need anything from your place, give me a list. I'll make sure you get it. It's not safe for you to be going back there. Deirdre, I need you to pack an emergency bag. I won't tell you what to take. You know better than me. You've been through this too many times before."

She nodded. She then spoke, "Who tells my parents about Finn? Do I or do you? They never really gave me a lot of support at the time and I can't figure out why. Ben and Marg were more support than them."

"We'll look after it for you, Deirdre. We'll have officers from their town go and talk to them. Your Dad is still overseas. We are going to try and keep him there. Your Mom we'll have placed somewhere safe. I know they have people who can run the mission while they're away."

Deirdre snorted. "Like they have ever been given a chance." The men looked at her. "My parents never leave the mission together. There is always one or the other in charge. Not ever do they leave anyone else in charge. That's the way it's always been. That's why I left and came to Ben and Marg. They have time for each person in their lives. If you're going through a storm, you need someone there with you. I didn't have that at home. I do here."

Chapter 11

Frankie was pacing. He knew Eddie and Caleb were working on a safe place, but how safe would it be? He could hear Deirdre in the kitchen. He wandered that way and stopped to watch her.

She looked up. "Here's a sandwich. I figured we may as well eat. Who knows when we'll next get a chance."

He studied her, then walked towards her. He took the plate from her hand and set it on the table, then reached to pull her into a hug. She stood stiff at first, then her arms came up and she hugged him back. He could feel the tears through his shirt. She just needed someone to hold her and let her mourn. She had much to mourn. Eddie had really thrown a lot at her today.

She stepped back, swiping at her eyes. He reached around her, wet a cloth and then gently washed her face. His hand lingered on her cheek, then she turned away.

"Eat up. Who know when Eddie will be back to take us who knows where."

"You need to eat too. I won't if you won't." Frankie watched until she finally made herself a sandwich and dropped herself into a chair. He poured them both cups of coffee and then sat down. He reached for her hand as he said a blessing on their food.

She tugged at her hand when he was done but he didn't release it. She looked up at him. "Don't say anything, Frankie. Just don't say anything."

"I don't intend to. The only thing I was going to say is what you tell me. God is here in the storm. He has called us to come and find rest in the midst of the turmoil. Will you remember that and run to Him?"

She lowered her eyes and then sighed. "Yes. It's just so hard."

"I know, darling, I know. Now eat up before you need to get scary with the bad guys." That earned him a smack on the arm.

****

The Watcher studied the house. He knew they were in there. He had not seen them leave. There were, however, police officers all around. There would not be an opportunity for him or his men to get to them. He would need to wait for that. But time was running out. He needed that information and quickly. Those two would pay for this delay and so would anyone else who got in his way.

****

Frankie sank down into a chair in the dim light of the living room and rested his head back. His gaze went to Deirdre. She had finally curled up under a blanket on the couch and dozed off. His heart broke for the woman he loved. She had been dealt such a blow or two today. He prayed for healing for her, for comfort, for strength, for protection. He prayed for safety for her family. He prayed for wisdom and safety of the law enforcement teams that were working around the clock. He felt like he was in a free fall with a parachute that may not open until too late.

Deirdre stirred slightly in her sleep. He could tell it wasn't restful. His eyes slid shut and he slept as well. He had been running on empty he felt for so long and he just couldn't not sleep.

Frankie stirred as he heard Caleb and Eddie enter. Ben was with them. Ben stopped by the couch and stared down at his niece. Frankie saw the sadness in his face and understood that he had been told about Finn.

Frankie headed to the kitchen with Caleb and Eddie. They spoke in low tones, then turned as Ben entered the room.

"Are we set?" Caleb asked.

"I think so." Eddie looked around. "Are you two ready to go?"

"About as ready as we can be." Frankie hesitated. "Before we go, can we pray?"

The four men bowed their heads and Ben led them to God's throne. Frankie walked away from that prayer humbled by the power of God he could feel in the room. Who knew what was coming next but God did and God was in control.

Ben touched his niece's shoulder and called her name. She stirred and then sat up. He sat beside her and gathered her close for a few minutes like he would a daughter. They had a few minutes of soft whispered conversation. Then Ben stood.

"We're set. The plan is in place?"

"It is and hopefully we can throw off those men until we can find them."

Lights went off in the house and Frankie and Deirdre were led out through the garage to a car waiting inside. Two officers who resembled them in height and build went into the house and then out the front door with Eddie and Caleb. They hustled them to a waiting car and then left, escort cars in place. Ben waited patiently. They were in no rush.

Finally word came from Eddie that they were being followed. Ben climbed behind the wheel of Deirdre's car.

He turned to the two. "Down on the floor on the back seat. We want it to look as if it's just me case someone has remained behind. No one will question me taking your car, Deirdre, if you're on the run, which is what we have tried to put across. They know I was with Caleb and Eddie and that they left with you two."

Ben backed out of the garage and then hit the remote to shut it. He looked around, didn't see anyone and drove off. He seemed to be driving around in circles but in fact he was watching for tails. Not seeing any, he headed for his next destination, the impound yard at the department. He drove up to the gate and then punching in his password, entered. He drove to the very end of the lot and stopped.

"Just stay down and wait," he cautioned. "We still don't know if they followed us."

Frankie moved restlessly. Crouching in the back seat of a car didn't sit well with his almost six-foot frame. Deirdre reached out for his hand and he clasped hers in his. How long they had waited, he didn't know, but finally Ben moved.

Ben turned slightly to speak with them. "You are going to get out on the passenger side and get behind that truck over there. Wait for me once you do. I'm going to move Deirdre's car and park it well out of sight. I'll be back." He looked around again, and then said, "Move."

Frankie slid the door opened and grabbing his pack, pulled Deirdre with him and out of sight. He hoped Ben was right and no one was around. He could feel the hair on his neck rising once again. Not now, Lord, he prayed. Let us please get away. Keep us safe. He could feel Deirdre's hand on his back. They waited.

A soft sound came to them and they tensed.

"Frankie, Deirdre." It was Ben. "It looks clear. Come on, let's get you out of here." He led them to another vehicle, an older beat up sedan. "Don't worry about the looks. It's got lots of power under the hood." When they were inside, he spoke, "Stay down on the floor until we get out of here. There's a blanket to cover yourselves with."

Frankie reached for the blanket, then his hand stopped. "What else is back here?"

"Just a couple of garbage bags stuffed with paper to keep it light. Part of the disguise."

Frankie grumbled under his breath. Deirdre laughed softly.

"Behave yourself, Franklin, or I'll find my scary friends."

Ben shook his head at their nonsense. They did need some levity in the situation but he really wasn't sure if this was the time.

He pulled up to the gate and punching in code once again, pulled through. He scanned the area. So far, so good. It didn't look as if anyone had seen them. Now to go to Part B of Caleb's plan.

****

The Watcher stood in Deirdre's house. He had managed to get in and had walked through the entire place. She was not here. It didn't look like she had been for a while, but his men were adamant they had followed her here. And that man was with her as well. He had stood and watched. He was sure that it was not them who had been taken away with the escort. Who had taken her out of his clutches once again? Fists raised to the heavens, he cursed. Someone would pay and pay dearly. Now, who would he start with?

****

Ben pulled up to the curb in front of a coffee shop and looked around. He didn't see anyone but he would wait for a bit.

"You can pull the blanket off, but stay down as much as you can. Be ready to cover back up if you have to."

"What the plan, Ben?" Frankie wanted to know.

"You'll find out soon. Caleb should be here soon. First, let me have your phones. They're finding you when they shouldn't be. Next, your backpacks will be staying in this car. We have other ones for you to take with you."

Frankie nodded. "That makes sense. They've been in our homes. They could very easily have planted tracking devices. I am assuming you swept for bugs?"

Ben nodded, barely visible in the dim light. "We did. We didn't find anything."

Frankie thought about that. "Then it is likely our phones. I wondered why they didn't take them from us. That just never made any sense."

"No, it never did. I'll have one of our techs go over them. Here, put these in your shoes." Ben handed over tiny devices. "They'll let us track you, but they won't be able to. We won't lose you." Ben sighed. "Deirdre, how sure are you that the men are from overseas?"

She stared at him as she thought about what he asked. "Their accents were right on. I guess it doesn't mean they're from overseas. I assumed and now that assumption is coming back to haunt me. Do you have proof they're not?"

"That's what we're running with right now. Whoever is after you is not from that country. It wouldn't make sense for them to have hired men from overseas and brought them here. It would make more sense to have found thugs here and then used them. We're working on that angle."

"Whoever they are, they certainly are stereotypical. But it has never made sense. Why target us?"

"We've determined that you're the target. Frankie is collateral. They won't really care if either of you live once they get the information they need."

Deirdre shuddered. Frankie reached for her hand as she said, "That is just plain sick."

Car lights crossed their vehicle and Frankie reached to pull the blanket over them once again. Ben pulled away from the curb and followed the car.

Frankie could smell the water as they pulled in. They were near the lake. Ben climbed out of the car and walked away. They heard his footsteps come back and then the back door of the car opened.

"Come on, you two. We have another mode of transportation waiting for you."

Frankie looked around as he turned to help Deirdre. He kept hold of her hand as they followed Ben towards the dock. A small cabin cruiser was waiting there.

"No, don't tell me. You're really not, are you?" Deirdre's face was pale. "I can't do that."

Ben looked at her with compassion. "You can and you will. It may be the only means we have to keep you alive." He sighed and looked up. "I know how hard it will be but you need to. Besides you can put on your scary face and scare all the fish away."

Frankie laughed softly at her outraged cry, then watched in amazement as she straightened her shoulders and walked toward the boat.

Ben watched her. "Marg and I have never been able to figure out her fear of boats. She can swim, canoe, kayak, but don't ask her to get on a boat. She flat out refuses, or did until today." Ben looked at Frankie. "She's doing it for you, to keep you alive."

Frankie stared at Ben, then at Deirdre. He nodded. That made sense, she would do whatever she had to for those in her circle of family and friends.

"We're taking you across the lake to an island. We're hoping this way, they don't find you. But they always seem to. Eddie will be with you. We've also had a couple of fellows come in from a neighbouring department to help. That way it's not obvious we've pulled men from ours."

Frankie thought about that. "What about the youth centre? Who's keeping it going?"

"The board met. They have asked Peter, her assistant, to step up for now. He's good with the kids, almost as good as she is. He's really ready to take over if she ever decided she wanted out."

"Can't see that happening," Frankie replied.

"I know her. She's distancing herself, getting ready to step back. It's how she works. Come on, let's get you away from here."

****

The man stepped from the shadows and watched as the boat pulled away from the shore. He had found them. He just didn't know where they were headed. It had to be somewhere along the lake shore. He would search until he did find them. Then he would let the Watcher know. They would pay a handsome price for their trouble.

Chapter 12

Frankie wandered through the cottage they had been tucked away in. He still didn't feel safe. He knew Deirdre was still sleeping, he had checked on her about an hour ago. Eddie was somewhere around, likely outside doing his rounds. The two officers assigned to them were also around. He knew them slightly but not well. He prayed Caleb hadn't made a mistake in bringing them in.

Frankie finally sank into an easy chair and stared at the fireplace. It was a warm day but he envisioned the flickering flames that could illuminate that area. His head went back and he found himself lost in thought.

What had happened to his father? He just disappeared one day. His mother never talked about him much. Then one day, he came home to find his mother was gone as well. At least she left him a note, telling him she had to leave, that there was something only she could take care of. He always wondered where she was and if she was okay. There were times he felt very lonely. Maybe that's why he had been such a good cop on the street—he knew how they felt. He decided that when this whole thing going on right now was over he would try and track her down, just to make sure she was fine.

He turned his head as he heard a door shut. Eddie had come in from the outside and stopped to pour himself a cup of coffee. He looked over at Frankie, then poured a second one. He handed it to him, then sat down in the other easy chair.

"Everything okay?" Frankie asked, watching Eddie closely.

"So far, it seems to be. But I just don't know. Something feels off."

Frankie nodded. He knew that feeling. "I have the same feeling."

It had been a long day. Night had fallen. Deirdre looked around the cottage and sighed. This just wasn't home. She wanted to be home so badly, to go back to her kids at the centre. She just wanted this to be over and who knew how much longer it would continued. She watched Frankie and Eddie talking in the kitchen, solemn looks on their faces. They were worried, but hadn't talked to her yet about their worries. She looked around once more and then grabbing her Bible headed for the bedroom she had been assigned. Spending time in the Bible and prayer just seemed to be the right thing to do.

Frankie looked up as her door clicked shut. He hadn't been avoiding her but he just wanted to know what was going on and what Caleb and Ben were planning. Eddie wasn't saying much but he did say they were working on the mystery and had good leads. He hoped that soon they would uncover who was behind the abduction and make an arrest.

Eddie stretched. It had been a long day and wasn't over yet. He was still waiting to hear from Caleb or Ben. Like Frankie, he wasn't too sure of the other officers—he had never worked with them before and these were friends he was trying to protect.

One of the officers entered. "All clear, so far. How did you want to work the night shift?"

Eddie thought and then said, "If we take two hours shifts, we'll all get some kind of rest. I'll take the first watch. You two get some sleep. It's going to be a long few days and we need to conserve our energy."

The other man nodded and then looked around.

Eddie spoke. "There's a bedroom at the end of the room. It has twin beds. You two can have it. I'll bunk in with Frankie when I need to."

Frankie watched as the man headed for the bedroom. He could feel a presence around him that he didn't like.

Eddie's eyes fell on Frankie and he stopped. "What's up, Frankie?"

Frankie shook his head. "I don't know, I really don't. Just that feeling. I used to get it on the street."

Eddie nodded. "You never lose that sense even when you stop being a street cop or undercover. It's yours for life. I have the same feeling, that something is about to happen, and we can't stop it." He clapped Frankie on the shoulder. "Go, get some rest."

****

The two men silently beached their canoe. They had come prepared to take those two with them. It really didn't matter to them if others died in the process. It would be messy, but messy was how they lived. They gestured to each other and then approached the cabin, splitting up to each take a side. A quick movement and the guard went down.

They approached the cabin on silent feet and cautiously opened the door. The main room was empty. They crept in and listened at the doors. They opened one— Frankie lay asleep. With silent gestures, they approached the bed.

Frankie's eyes flew open as he felt a presence in the room. A quick blow and he was rendered helpless. One of the men slung him over his shoulder and walked cautiously back out. The other headed for another room. Peeking in he saw it was the officers, sound asleep. He went to the next room, cautiously opening the door. It was Deirdre's room. He once again approached the bed. She didn't stir. A quick movement with a cloth and bottle and he knew she wouldn't. He gathered her up and left.

****

Eddie stirred at hands shook him, pain radiating through his skull. What had happened? Hands helped him to sit and then to rise. Once in the cabin, he sank into a chair, trying to figure out what was going on. He raised pain-filled eyes to see Caleb standing in front of him. His eyes slid closed. Not again, he thought, please not again. My heart can't take it, not being able to protect my friends.

Caleb crouched in front of him. "Eddie, are you okay? No, don't shake your head. It will make it hurt worse than it is. You had a heavy blow."

"Frankie and Deirdre?"

Caleb shook his head. "They're gone. Whoever took them is good. Not a sound. We did find evidence in Deirdre's room that she was drugged."

Eddie stared at Caleb. "I'm getting tired of this, Caleb. How are we supposed to protect them? We do our best and they still get found."

Caleb stood and nodded. "I know. I just wish I knew how. Ben's working that angle. I hate to tell him Deirdre's missing again."

Eddie drew a deep breath. "That is not going to be fun. How's the investigation going?"

Caleb was silent and Eddie just watched him. More was going on that what Caleb was ready to say. Caleb sighed and then turned to sit.

"It's really getting messy. The ones involved would not be who you expected." He turned to look at Eddie and started stating names. Eddie's face showed his shock.

"Never saw those coming."

"None of us did. This is really going to hurt when it comes out."

"What about the two officers from the other town? Are they okay?"

Caleb nodded. "They are. I don't know how they didn't hear anything though. They slept right through it until morning. They realized you hadn't come to wake them, went looking, found you and then Frankie and Deirdre missing. I was already on my way over when I got the call."

"You've done your best, Caleb."

"I know but it sure doesn't feel like it." Caleb was frustrated. He now had to try and track where Frankie and Deirdre were. They could be anywhere and his gut told him they were running short of time. "Hannah did give me a name."

Eddie stilled and watched Caleb. He could tell it was not what he would want to hear. At the name, his eyes closed. No, it wasn't possible. Caleb was right. This was really going to hurt and hurt bad.

"Come on, Eddie. Let's get you home and get your head looked at. It's going to be a long few days, I think."

"It will. I feel like we're in the middle of a cat 5 hurricane or and EF5 tornado. Just have to keep remembering that Christ calmed the storm on Galilee. He will calm this storm too."

****

The Watcher stood in the dimness of the hall and watched aa the two who had tried to elude him were carried in and down the stairs to the basement. Soon, he would have want he wanted. Soon, he would be able to destroy those who had tried to stop him. Soon. He felt victorious.

Chapter 13

Frankie moaned as he tried to move. His head hurt and he didn't remember running into anything. His eyes cracked open and shut again. The light was just too bright. He tried opening them again and this time he could focus. He looked around and then up. A basement, he thought. A room in the basement. There would be no way they could get out of the windows. They were small.

He rolled over onto his back. The pounding in his head was easing off some. He didn't see Deirdre. He sat up quickly and then regretted it at the fresh pounding behind his eyes. He scanned the room. She wasn't there. Where was she?

He staggered as he came to his feet, caught his balance and headed for the door. The knob turned under his hand and he pulled the door open. Cautiously, he stopped through. Deirdre was laying on the floor, not moving. Heart sinking, he stumbled to his knees beside her and reached out a hand. She was alive. Thank you, God, he whispered.

He looked around. He needed to find a way out of these rooms and soon. The windows weren't much of an option—they were small. The door opposite him was locked and he doubted that Deirdre would still have her knife, if the men had done their job right this time. Walls were solid.

He sank back to the floor near Deirdre, despair in his being. There was just no way out. He looked at the ceiling and prayed. God, You know where we are. You have a way out. Calm the storm within me and help me to think.

The sound of the door unlocking caught his attention. He turned. A larger man stood there. He recognized him as one of the men from before. Nothing was said as a tray of food was set down. The man's hard gaze locked with his own. Frankie could barely contain the shudder he felt at the evil in that gaze. The man backed away and locked the door once again.

Frankie laid his head back on the wall. At least for now, it looked as if they wanted them to stay alive if they were bringing in meals. He had no desire to eat. He raised his head and studied the tray. There were cups of fluid, what he couldn't tell from where he sat, but he wasn't prepared to even taste them and he wouldn't let Deirdre either.

Deirdre stirred. She had a dry bad taste in her mouth. She wondered where she was. It didn't feel like the bed she had laid down on last night. She sat up, then waited as her head steadied. She looked around and saw Frankie sitting beside her, eyes on her.

"Where are we?" She had to clear her voice to continue. "What happened?"

Frankie watched her, then sighed. "You're not going to like it. We're back in the hands of those men."

"How?"

"That's what I want to know. Something failed in the security somewhere along the line."

"So now what?"

Frankie shrugged. "I don't see a way out of here. Windows are too small. That door over there is locked. No other openings in the wall."

"Did you get a look at anyone?"

"Just the one who brought in a tray of food."

"Food?"

He nodded. "Food and drink. It looks as if they want to keep us alive, at least for now." He paused and then continued, "But we're not eating the food or drinking whatever is in those cups. I won't take a chance on them being drugged or poisoned."

"How long do you think we've been here, wherever here is?"

"Going by the sun, I'd say it's around 10 in the morning. So sometime after midnight I would suspect, maybe eight hours?"

Deirdre stood and walked around the room they were in and then into the room Frankie had awakened in.

"Frankie, come here."

Frankie followed her voice. She was standing at the far end of the room, running her hand down the wall. "It sounds hollow behind here. I wonder what's back here."

"It's a solid wall, Deirdre."

She shook her head. "No, it looks like it's just drywall. We could try some fancy moves and kick through it."

Frankie stared at her. "Kick our way through? Seriously? Deirdre, you have no idea what's on the other side of that."

She nodded. "I know, but we really could find out. It may be the opening out we need."

He shook his head, grabbed her hand and pulled her away. "We'll talk about that. By the way, do you still have your knife?"

She felt her pockets. "I do."

He stared at her again. "You do? They cleaned out our pockets." He stopped, then waved his hands. "I really don't want to know. Your scary friends again right?"

She smacked his arm. "My friends are scary. They have knowledge that they were willing to share. They're scholars in the university of life."

Frankie shook his head as he followed her from the room. "We'll think about that wall, scary one. Right now, come sit down. We need to pray. God will provide us a way."

Deirdre looked at him and nodded. "That He will. But are we prepared for the way He may take?"

Frankie's eyes sought her. He read in hers the realization she had come to. Like him, she wondered if they would make it out alive.

Deirdre suddenly felt for her shoes. "Do you still have it?"

Frankie looked at her in surprise.

"Do you still have it? What Ben gave us?"

His eyes brightened and he felt for his shoe. He nodded.

She sat back. "Good."

Frankie and Deirdre stared at each other. Caleb could track them but would it be in time?

Chapter 14

Caleb stood looking around the conference room. It was a frenzy of activity. He had officers tracking the men they suspected of the abduction, other verifying facts for the case. Another two were on a computer, trying to trace the GPS units Ben had given them.

He turned as Eddie came up and stood beside him.

"I feel so frustrated, Caleb. This should not have happened."

"I know, Eddie. It shouldn't. Those two officers will have some hard questions to answer."

"How's Ben taking this?"

Caleb sought for words. "Not well, I'm afraid. His faith is shaking right now. I sent him home to Marg. I gather Beth is heading this way too. Haven't heard about Brett though."

"Brett. Now there's someone I would really like to talk to. He had better have some good answers when I do."

"All in good time, Eddie, all in good time."

Caleb moved away from Eddie towards the officers search for the GPS tracking.

"What do we have, Megan?"

"Provided they still have their shoes on, here's the address. They're not moving from there, but I am picking up some subtle shifting."

"Thank you, Megan. You may have just saved their lives."

Caleb turned and searched the room. Finding who he wanted, he crossed to the ETF leader. "Doug, get your men ready. Here's the address we think they're at." Caleb quickly scrawled it for him. "Get out there and let me know what you find. I'll be there as soon as I can get everything organized from here."

Doug nodded and then looked up. "We'll find them, Caleb. Frankie has been there more than once when we had situations in the down town area. We'll bring them home."

Frankie and Deirdre turned to watch as the door opened. They were resigned to whatever was happening. They just prayed their friends would find them quickly. The door swung back against the wall, and the two men who had abducted them stood there.

Deirdre's breath caught softly as the next man entered. Her fingers grasped Frankie's tightly.

Nothing was said as he studied the two. Frankie could feel evil shimmering all around his body. He knew Deirdre was tense, he could feel it. Why he didn't know.

Then, Deirdre spoke. "Meet Finn's father, Frankie. Stu McNabb."

Frankie shot a look at her and then back to the man.

"Still have your attitude, I see, Deirdre. Finn hated that about you."

Deirdre was shaking her head. "No, actually, he didn't. You did. You did because I refused to back down from you each and every time we had a confrontation. So tell me. Did you have your son killed?

Were you the one who insisted on the wedding that wasn't a wedding?"

McNabb stared at her. "The wedding that wasn't a wedding? Oh no, my dear, it was a legitimate wedding."

Deirdre was shaking her head. "No, actually, it wasn't. Friends of mine have proof it wasn't. Finn was planning on running that day, and you knew it. You had him killed to stop him." She studied him. "Just how deep does this go?"

Frankie was worried. She was baiting the man and he looked as if he was ready to snap.

McNabb was shaking his head. "You know nothing, my dear. Absolutely nothing. Now, you are going to answer questions for me. The life of your friend there depends on it."

She was shaking her head. "No, I don't think so. I have no idea what you want. None whatsoever."

The older man stared at her. She stared back. This was the father of the man she thought she had loved and who she thought had loved her. It was all a sham.

She could see the changes in him, changes wrought by evil and greed. She was not ready to go down without a fight, and she knew Frankie was the same.

Caleb stood near Doug. "You're sure they're in there?"

"Pretty sure. The vehicles you had tagged are there. Megan says the GPS is still reading here. We'll have to go in to make sure."

Caleb nodded. "I have warrants on the way, just to be nice and legal. I don't want any loopholes to trip us up."

"Wise move. I'll give you a heads up when we're ready to move in."

Ben stopped beside Caleb. "Any word yet?"

Caleb shook his head. "You shouldn't be here, Ben."

"No, I need to be. That's my niece in there. I'll stay back out of the way, but I need to be here."

"Has Beth arrived?"

"Not yet but she was almost here. Timothy came home. He refused to stay away."

"I thought he might. He's too much like his father. How's Marg handling it?"

Ben gave a small smile. "She's on her knees, Caleb. She's on her knees. She's also called the prayer chain and set that in motion."

Caleb nodded as he looked around. Eddie was headed his way.

"I'm sorry, Ben." Eddie's voice broke into Ben's thought. "I wasn't able to stop them."

Ben turned to study his friend. "No, you couldn't, Eddie. There are only two men here on earth who can, and they don't appear willing to stop this. God is allowing it to happen, only He knows why."

Ben stopped, unable to continue. Caleb and Eddie shared a glance, then turned to watch the activity quietly unfolding in front of them.

Frankie was pulled to his feet and shoved through the door into the adjoining room. The door slammed shut. Deirdre watched, then turned eyes to McNabb. She was getting really frightened but struggled to control it.

"Don't worry, my dear. He will be fine."

Deirdre shook her head. "I doubt it. I'm beginning to see just how depraved you are."

The man's lips curled back in anger, then he smoothed out his face. "I don't think so. I am not depraved. I just want what is mine."

The two men entered and Deirdre caught just a glimpse of Frankie's crumpled form. Please, Lord, let him live. I don't care about me, but let him live.

"Stand up, my dear. You have some questions to answer."

Deirdre looked at him and shook her head. "I have nothing to answer. I don't have whatever it is you're looking for."

He stared at her, anger beginning to rise within him. He motioned to the two men, who hauled her to her feet and held her tightly.

"That, my dear, was a mistake. You will pay for your defiance."

He stepped towards her. "Where are the stones?"

"What stones?" Deirdre was good, she knew how to keep a calm, clear face in times of danger.

"You know exactly what stones I want."

She shook her head. "I don't have them. I have no idea where they are."

He stared at her, then motioned to one of his men. Deirdre had a feeling things were just about to get worse and she wasn't going to like them much. Her heart lifted to God for strength and protection.

Doug headed back to Caleb. "We got imaging up. We have four in the basement right now. The fifth one has come back upstairs." He listened to his radio for a minute. "No, we have three upstairs now. It's your call, Caleb."

Caleb studied the house, and then nodded. "When you're ready. It's your call as to when and how but we need to do this."

Caleb hadn't asked about the other two, Doug noted. He was worried. Imaging was showing that the two forms in the basement weren't moving.

Doug's team moved in silently and quickly. They breached the doors and were inside before the three men knew what was happening. A flurry of activity and the three were handcuffed and being led out of the house.

Stu McNabb stared in hatred at Caleb. "This is unwarranted. I'll have your badge and your job."

Caleb held up his warrants. "We wouldn't have these if it was unwarranted. The judge agreed with us. We have you on solid evidence, McNabb. Get him out of here."

Caleb strode towards the house. The ETF team was finishing clearing it. Doug appeared at the door and yelled for paramedics. Caleb stepped to the side to watch, Eddie coming up beside him.

"I am praying that means they're still alive, Caleb."

"Me, too, Eddie. Where's Ben?"

"He waiting by your car. He won't come in until and unless you call him. He doesn't want anything to be said that would hinder your case against McNabb."

Caleb nodded. "Let him know I'll be back out as soon as I can. Round up your evidence teams, Eddie. I know you have them waiting back there."

Caleb stepped into the opulent house. He looked around and felt sorrow building up in him. Money that should have gone for good had ended up in the pockets of a greedy, depraved man. Lives had been changed and ruined because of him.

He looked up to see Doug approaching, a grim look on his face. His heart sank. Were they too late?

"They're alive, Caleb. They're alive but not in great shape. I was just coming to find you."

Caleb followed Doug down the stairs and into the rooms in the basement. He stopped as he saw Deirdre's crumpled form on the floor. She had taken a beating and a bad one he assumed. He stepped around the paramedics working on her to the doorway of the next room. Another team was working on Frankie. He could see he had been beaten severely as well. They were getting ready to place him on the stretcher when he heard his name called.

He turned and walked back to where they were working on Deirdre. He heard a whimper from her as her hand was moved, and tears started to trickle down her face. He crouched down beside the head paramedic.

A gasp from the other side caught his attention and he looked. The younger paramedic had a look of horror on his face. "They really didn't, did they? They really didn't break her fingers?"

Caleb's eyes shot to her right hand. Dave, the senior paramedic, was gently holding her wrist and cradling her hand. He nodded. "They did. I want to get my hands on them." Dave looked sick at what he was seeing. Caleb knew he had served overseas as a medic and had seen things he wouldn't talk about. This was really hitting him hard. "I need a splint, then we can get an IV started, get her loaded and on her way."

Caleb reached to brush a tear from Deirdre's face. He really didn't know how he felt right now. He stood and looked around. If there had been something to kick, he just might have kicked it. He struggled to control the nausea he felt. He watched as the team carried Frankie past and up the stairs. He knew he needed to go too, but he wanted to wait for Deirdre. He wanted to be the one who talked to Ben.

Chapter 15

Ben stood and watched as they loaded Frankie's stretcher in the ambulance and then left, police escort in place. He turned to watch the house, waiting for Deirdre to come out, waiting for Caleb to come to talk to him, just waiting. His heart sank as he tried to imagine what was going on. No one was saying much. He lifted his eyes and prayed harder than he had in a long time.

Eddie stepped through the door and came to stand by Caleb. He studied the men working on Deirdre and then saw the splint on her hand.

"No," he said. "They didn't, did they?"

Caleb nodded. "They did. Dave figures two fingers and at least one bone of the third. How she stood that, I'll never know."

Eddie looked sick and he had to turn away. They had both seen some very cruel things on the job, but he thought this just might be the worse. "How do we tell Ben, and then her family?"

Caleb shook his head. "I have no idea, Eddie."

He watched as they carried her up the stairs and through the house to the stretcher waiting outside. He stepped past them and saw Ben headed for him. He reached out and stopped Ben with a hand on his chest.

Ben stared past him at his niece, then at Caleb.

"She's alive?"

Caleb nodded. "She is. She's had a bad beating, as has Frankie. There's something else, though, Ben." He stopped unable to continue for a minute. Ben's eyes bore into his. "They broke fingers on her hand, more than likely to get her to talk."

Ben's eyes closed, then an angry look covered his face. He pushed past Caleb to where his niece lay. He reached out a hand and touched her hair. At a word from the paramedics, he stepped back and watched them move to the waiting ambulance. He followed and climbed in before the doors closed, without speaking a word.

Caleb watched, then turned to Eddie. "Go, follow them. Stick with him. I don't know what he's thinking."

Eddie nodded and headed for his car. This was one of the hardest times he could ever remember. He knew Marg and Beth would be brought to the hospital. Timothy would be as well.

Caleb finally was able to make his way to the hospital. He was bone-deep weary, almost ready to drop in his tracks. Today had been one of the hardest days he had ever faced. He searched the waiting room and saw Hannah with Marg and Beth. Timothy sat near them. Caleb saw his brother, Joshua, there and knew Hannah had called him to come sit with Timothy. He nodded. She was wise, his wife, knowing what to ask for and do almost before he had framed the thought.

Eddie met him and motioned him back outside.

"What's the word, Eddie?"

Eddie stared across the parking lot. Officers were milling around inside and out, there to provide support for their own.

"Frankie is still unconscious. They did a number on him, that's for sure. Bruised, if not fractured ribs. His left wrist is fractured. The doctors think he has a concussion. They're waiting for imaging results."

"And Deirdre?"

Eddie had trouble speaking, then drew in a breath. "How can they treat a woman like that? The doctors said much more of a beating, she would be dead. Even now they're not sure what effect the beating will have. Her hand—they have her in surgery right now trying to do reconstruction on it. They have no idea if they can fix it or if she'll have good movement in those fingers." He stopped, having to control his emotions. "Who in their right mind does that?"

"They're not in their right mind, Eddie. That's the problem." Caleb looked behind him into the Emergency department. "Where do they have Frankie?"

"Room 6 right now." He stopped. "Deirdre's dad is on his way back. Beth figures he'll be here tomorrow."

Caleb nodded. "Thanks. Go home, Eddie, go home to Peggy. You need some rest. Spend time in prayer with your wife."

Eddie stood for a time, then nodded. "You need to rest too, Caleb. Hannah's here. Go, be with her."

"I will, once I find out how Frankie is."

Eddie started to walk away, then stopped and turned to face Caleb. "She can't have said anything. Most people, including men, would have caved at the first bone. They were at two and a half fingers with her." Having said that, he turned and walked away.

Caleb stared at him, lost in thought. He was right. She hadn't given them what they wanted. He shook his head. Frankie, you have a very special lady there, I hope you know that.

Later, Caleb stood at Frankie's bedside. He had been moved to a private room. His face was battered as were his hands. His left wrist was in a cast. Caleb studied his friend. Once again he was struck with how man's depravity would show itself.   Lives lost, beatings, theft, greed. When would it end?

He knew there would be a guard at Frankie's door. He still wasn't sure they had everyone involved in custody.   There had been many volunteers. His department was reeling from this. Men and women both had volunteered to watch Deirdre's room.   He knew men and women were in the waiting room. He still felt helpless.

He went to find Ben. Ben had refused to go home.   He had sent Marg, Beth and Timothy back home.   Beth had not argued and Caleb found that real strange. He knew if that had been Hannah, nothing and no one would have made her leave.

He found Ben outside, sitting at a picnic table provided for the staff breaks. He sat across from him, not saying anything.

"Why, Caleb? Why?" Ben anguished voice caught at Caleb.

Caleb shook his head.   "It's coming together, Ben. We're working through it all. There was a lot of evidence gathered from McNabb's office today.   We need to work through that." Caleb stopped speaking. "It's going to get a lot messier, Ben."

Ben nodded. "I know."

Caleb stood, laid his hand on his friend. "I won't tell you to go home; I know it won't do any good. Get some sleep if you can. Call me if you need to. I'm heading home but I'll be back in the morning." Caleb walked away before Ben could speak.

Chapter 16

Morning came too soon as far as Caleb was concerned. He was at the office almost before he felt he had slept any. The investigation was really ramping up. His team was good and they were ferreting out information McNabb thought he had hidden away permanently.

After spending time with the investigators, Caleb headed for the hospital. This was going to be one of those days, and Caleb didn't feel ready for it.

He went to check on Frankie, figuring this was going to be the easier of the tasks. He nodded at the officer at the door and then pushed the door open to enter. He stopped at the side of the bed and watched his friend. Still out of it, he guessed, or sleeping, he couldn't tell. He winced at the bruising and cuts he saw. He thanked God that Frankie was still alive.

He turned and walked away towards Deirdre's room. He once more stopped at a bedside. Deirdre was heavily sedated he knew for the pain. He studied the bandages on her hand and wondered if they had been able to reconstruct it sufficiently so she would regain use of it. He studied her face next. He stayed there for a while, then walked away, walked towards the waiting room, a sense of foreboding in his thoughts.

He found Ben standing by himself, staring out the window. Caleb stopped beside him.

"How is she? I was just in there and she's still out."

Ben nodded. "They have her sedated, partly for the pain." Ben's eyes filled with tears. "I can't imagine the pain she must have been put through. The doctors said they were able to pretty much reconstruct the hand back to what it was. The little finger, they're not sure about. But one thing is for certain, she'll always have trouble with that hand. They didn't think there was nerve damage but they have to wait for the swelling to go down." Ben stopped speaking. "Why, Caleb? Why did those monsters think it was so worth while?"

Caleb shook his head. "I don't know, Ben. We're trying to get that information, but we're in early stages yet. I'm sorry about Brett. I had no idea when all this started that he would be involved."

Ben's eyes slid shut in sorrow. "I didn't either. I knew he had been changing over the years, not the same as when we grew up. When Deirdre went through what she did and came to us, he never came after her. He never called. Never wrote. Just went on as if it didn't matter. I guess it really didn't. Eddie was over late last night and let me know how that part of the investigation is going. I've stepped back from it so I won't compromise any of it. You were wise not to involve me in that part." Ben stopped, then turned to face the waiting room, his eyes seeking out his sister-in-law. "What part did Beth have?"

"We're still working on that part as well. Once we can get it all figured out, then we'll move with charges. Unfortunately, we have to arrest Brett now. I have officers waiting here with the warrant."

Ben nodded. "I'm surprised he would even come, given what's happened."

"He has to. He needs to save face. He doesn't know what all is out in the open." Caleb watched his friend. Sorrow coursed through him as he thought of what was coming. Nothing could prevent the end to the steps Brett had put in motion years ago.

A figure at the waiting room door had Ben stiffening. Caleb looked up and saw it was Brett. Beth went to him, spoke to him and led him down the hall. Marg looked over at Ben and then came to him. He wrapped his arm around her.

"How is Beth taking this?"

"Strangest thing, Ben. She's not concerned. It's as if Deirdre is a stranger's child. Doesn't make sense."

Caleb had a thought and excused himself. He went to find Eddie; he knew he was around here somewhere. A few words and Eddie had left, on his way to do some more research. Both had suspicions and Eddie was determined to prove them.

About thirty minutes later, Brett and Beth returned from their daughter's room. Caleb studied them. There was just something not there. They didn't have that concern about them they should.

Brett spoke with Marg and then turned to Ben. He stopped in front of Ben and reached out his hand to shake hands. Ben took one look, his fist came back, and Brett sprawled on the floor. Movement stopped in the waiting room, then Caleb reached down and hauled Brett to his feet.

"That was from your brother, not from a cop. This is from a cop." Caleb drew Brett's hands behind him and slapped on the handcuffs.

"What is this outrage?" Brett demanded.

"Well for starters, you're under arrest for conspiracy to commit murder, kidnapping, financial fraud, wire fraud, theft. I'm sure we'll find a few more charges before we're done"

Brett spluttered as he was led away. "I don't think so."

Beth watched dispassionately as he was led away. "I guess you'll be wanting to talk to me, too. We might as well get it over with." She followed her husband from the room.

Marg and Ben stared after them, then at each other. What had just happened?

Frankie rested his chin on the side bar of Deirdre's bed. It was four days later and she was gradually awakening from the medications she had been on. He himself still felt rocky. Two concussions in a short period of time was definitely not recommended.

His hand reached for her unbandaged hand and held it. This was the woman he had been waiting for. He thanked the Lord that He had spared her life.

Deirdre's eyelids flickered, and her eyes opened. Her sight was unfocused for a minute, then she frowned as she looked around. Her eyes went past him, then came back. She frowned as she studied his face.

"Who did you go twenty rounds with?" Her voice was rough, barely above a whisper.

He smiled. "Probably the same ones you did." She tried to lift her right hand and he reached across and stopped her. "Don't move that hand too much. They're waiting for it to heal more before they put it in a proper cast."

She frowned once more as she looked at it. "What happened to it?"

"You don't remember?" As she shook his head, he sighed. "The two goons with McNabb had a little fun with your hand. They decided to start breaking your fingers."

Her eyes flew to his. "I don't remember. Then again, maybe I don't want to. I imagine it must have hurt."

He laughed softly. "That, my darling, would be an understatement. The doctors are confident they've been able to reconstruct the fingers."

"So why else am I here?"

"Shock, dehydration, pain management. They were really starting to work you over before they decided to go for your fingers."

She loosened her left hand from his grip and touched his face. "Looks like you didn't fare as well, either."

"Not really.   Concussion again, fractured ribs, bruises, muscle trauma, broken wrist. But we're alive. God brought us through that storm."

"That He did, my love, that He did." Her voice faded and she slept.   He sat watching, her hand in his until he was asked to leave so the nurses could take care of her. He would be back and soon.

Chapter 17

Caleb looked around at the people gathered around the yard at Ben's place. Eddie and Peg were there. Joshua and Laycee, Leith and Regan, Liam and Ashling, Timothy. He knew Hannah was somewhere but their boys were with a friend. Ben and Marg had wanted to do this, have their friends over, just for a time to heal and pray. His eyes focused on the swing on the deck. Frankie was sitting there, his arm around Deirdre. Now that was a story in itself. Who would have thought that Frankie would have found such a wonderful soul mate, one to spend the rest of his life with, one who understood where he had been and where he was going? Only God.

The meal over, Caleb went to lean against the deck railing and faced his friends. This was one story that had so many twists and turns, he wasn't sure if they had unraveled them all.

He studied Deirdre. Her face was peaceful and calm. She had an inner strength he found in few. Her head was leaning back on Frankie's shoulder, his arm around her. He scanned the others, all focused on him.

Caleb started. "This is one story I'm not sure if we will ever totally unravel. It starts way back when you were small, Deirdre. Did you ever suspect your parents weren't your parents?"

She stared at him and shook her head. "Never."

"They weren't. They weren't able to have children on their own. They contacted a baby broker, what we would call a black market adoption today. He found them a little girl who matched them in looks. That was you. From what we have been able to determine, you were on a boat with your parents, it capsized, but somehow you survived. You were rescued, found yourself in this man's hands, and then on to Brett and Beth. That's why they didn't come around for a couple of years and let on that Beth was pregnant. Ben, you may recall they never really told you where the "baby" was born, did they? They didn't want you to know Beth wasn't pregnant.

"Then they started their mission. It started out on the right feet but somewhere along the line, Brett was corrupted and began stealing and selling the donations. Beth knew and at times helped. They made sure one or the other of them was always on site so no one would have access to the financials. They kept two books. Timothy, you were catching on. That's why Beth insisted you come back home.

"Stu McNabb was the silent partner in the criminal activities. He had been a childhood friend of Brett. Brett had lost track of him until he showed up one day and threatened him. Brett caved and brought him in on the crimes. Stu had the idea that if Finn and Deirdre were married, Brett wouldn't cause any problems. Problem is, Finn really didn't want to get married. So he arranged a fake wedding, making sure it was kept small. He was planning on disappearing once they were registered at the hotel, but his father suspected something. The shots were to be warning shots only but the shooter had his own agenda and killed Finn. McNabb realized that he was under watch and had been very careful since then to watch himself.

"Finn had given you that stone, Deirdre, as a safety precaution. He planned to find you and get it back. The one you found, Timothy, McNabb dropped one day he was in the warehouse.

"The two men McNabb hired were from here. He had connections to some gangs and specifically searched for these men, thinking the language would throw everyone off. Frankie is right, Deirdre, you are scary. Your language ability helped to crack the case.

"That's about it, I think. Still some odds and ends to sort out but we pretty much have the case against them in order. And yes, they were tracking your phones and had inserted GPS units in your backpacks. That threw them when we traded them out. It was just a pure fluke that they found you. They were searching around the docks, thinking you may try to flee by boat, and saw you."

Small talk followed and then the friends started to disperse. Caleb went looking for Frankie and found he and Deirdre standing in the back yard, near the roses.

"Frankie, can I have a word?"

"Sure." Frankie shrugged. "It's okay if you talk in front of Deirdre if you want to."

Caleb studied his friends, then nodded. "About your father. I found out and have confirmed he was one of the men gunned down that day. He was going under a different name. I have spoken with people who knew him. He was trying his best to clean up and come back to find you. Your mother had found out and that's why she left. Your mother was in a bad motor vehicle accident on the way to confront him. She had to have a lot of plastic surgery. She didn't feel she could come back around you, not when she had been gone for so long. Eddie tracked her down." Caleb paused, looking at the business card in his hand. "Eddie has spoken with her. She gave him her card, told him if you ever felt ready, she would like to hear from you. She's really not that far away from you, never has been."

Frankie's eyes slid shut. Deirdre's arms came around him in a hug. "Thank you, Caleb. It hurts but now I know. Thank you, my friend."

Caleb walked away. Sometimes, he just hated that part of his job that meant he had to hurt people.

Frankie stayed silent. Deirdre watched him. He finally turned to her.

"Well, my darling, it's been quite the few weeks."

She nodded, waiting for him to continue.

"Will you go out on a real date with me? No police escorts, just you and me?"

She nodded. "I would like that. Now about the youth centre."

"What about it?"

"I'm stepping down from it. I can't continue there, not any more. Peter's ready and able to take over. I'll find something else to do, something I will enjoy so much more."

"A wise move, my darling. Come, let's get you home. Caleb wants me to come in and start desk duty tomorrow. He never did accept my resignation."

"I'm glad he didn't. You're too good a cop."

"So, will you teach me your scary moves so I can scare away thugs in a dark alley?" He laughed as she punched him in the stomach. "I love you too, my darling.

Epilogue

Frankie was nervous and that was not like him. He wiped damp hands on his jeans and then rang Deirdre's doorbell. It had been four months since their adventure ended. They were still waiting for the trials, but it looked as if McNabb and Deirdre's adoptive father would be going to prison for a long time. Her mother would be on probation for her part, due to a plea bargain. The mission they had started had been closed down, it could not continue.

Deirdre opened the door and stood in front of him, breaking into his thoughts. Yes, Lord, thank you for this lady.

He reached for her hand and she closed and locked the door behind her. They had spent many hours together, alone and with family.

He walked her towards the park in her neighbourhood. It was small but beautiful in lay out. It had become part of their routine, to walk there at least two or three times a week.

He drew her close to him and then down to sit on a bench. He wrapped an arm around her and then just sat.

"Who would have thought all that would have happened to us?" Deirdre's voice was hushed.

"I know. You were so right about the storm. We were both going through a bad one. God calmed it for us, brought us safely to shore."

She nodded. "Now what, Frankie? Where does God lead us?"

He thought about that. "Only He knows where He wants us or where we can serve. There will be many more storms in life but we know Who calms them. I can't imagine a life that didn't have One like that in it. When I thought I had lost you that day in the basement, I was devastated. I tried so hard to get back to you. God spoke through the pain. He let me know we would both survive, that He had plans for us we have no idea of."

He turned his head to watch her. She was staring out across the park, a thoughtful look on her face.

"You're right. Even with what I was facing, not knowing if you were still alive, He was there, right beside me. He could have stopped what was happening but He didn't. He calmed the storm within, not the storm without. Sometimes that's what He does. He doesn't want us fearful, not at peace. That's not who we are to be."

Frankie nodded. "You're right. He gives what we need at the time we need it. I have spoken with my mother in the last week. It was hard but we're talking."

He looked over her head and then back down. "Deirdre, I have come to know you over the last few months, have come to love who you are. You're not the scary person I tease you about being. I love that part of you, that part that makes you unafraid and able to keep your head and think in a crisis."

She had turned her head to watch him.

"Will you marry me, will you help to be my anchor, help to keep me grounded and safe?"

Her eyes filling with tears, she nodded. "I will. I love that about you as well. You are my protector, the one who keeps me safe."

He leaned over to kiss her, then leaned back. "Did you really say yes?"

She shoved him. "Keep that up, buster, and I'll get scary again." She held up her hand. "Now, let's go get that dinner you promised me. You driving or am I?" His keys were in her hands.

He laughed and hugged her as he reached for them. "Don't ever change, my darling, don't ever change. And if the Lord blesses us with a family, you can teach them to be scary too."

Deirdre smacked him, then leaned in for a kiss. "That, my love, I can do."

Dear Readers:

The Storm is written. How much of a storm are you facing this day? Do you trust the Christ to calm the storm? Do you trust Him to calm you instead?

Frankie is a beat-up street cop, worn out and ready to turn his back on everything. Deirdre enters his life and changes how he views himself and how he sees God as viewing him. God really does want us to trust in Him, to find that rest we need, to find the calm in our storms of life.

This book is dedicated to those of us, every one of us, who have fought through a storm and emerged victoriously through Christ's power. We don't need to wonder how it happened. That's where our faith comes in—that it will.

As always, I pray that this book has challenged you in your walk with God. It has me. I also pray that you really will learn to let God have control of your storms in life, to lay your worries, cares, stresses, and burdens in His outstretched hands.

Ronna